# Poison, She Chose.

by

Raymond Knight Read

# Poison, She Chose.

*The Professor George Wellbelove Investigates series.*

Copyright © Raymond Knight Read, 2016

All right reserved. No part of this publication may be reproduced, stored in a retrieval system, or transmitted in any form or by any means, electronic, mechanical, photocopying, recording or otherwise without prior permission of the author.

Also by the author:-

*Professor George Wellbelove Investigates series*

The Scent of Bitter Almonds – Locked Room Mysteries

Volume 1.

The Russian Pantomime – Locked Room Mysteries

Volume 2.

*Sauna Mortis* – Locked Room Mysteries

Volume 3.

Requiem for Harmonica and Shotgun – Locked Room Mysteries

Volume 4.

The Third Gunman


Operation Marigold

Krahgdahl – Run, But You Can't Escape

Atlantis Dimension *(coming soon)*

*And for Children*

Doctor Dog series:-

Doctor Dog

A Touch of Spring Fever

Summer Breezes, Autumn Leaves

Snow, Frost and Blue Lightning

Snow, Frost and Ice Cream

Close Encounters of the Monty-Kind *(coming soon)*

*All great literary edifices are built*

*On one wondrous and mystical foundation – inspiration*

*God bless inspiration.*

'Where can people hide poison bottles, George?' the Chief Inspector asked as he broke his digestive biscuit in half and dunked a corner into his cup of tea.

The Professor's eyes flicked up, but then returned to the fine gilt Mappin & Webb Victorian carriage clock that he was re-assembling on the desk in his study at home.

'Theoretically?' the Professor asked, 'Or are you subtly, or perhaps not very subtly, trying to drag me into one of your cases?' he smiled.

'A bit of both,' the Chief Inspector said dunking the second half of his biscuit.

The Professor grinned – he knew that was a clear "yes".

George had just taken all the brass gear-wheels, barrels and miscellaneous tiny parts out of his new ultrasonic cleaning machine that Dorothy, his wife, had bought him for his birthday.

With all the parts refurbished, George was anxious to re-assemble the carriage clock – but the task required his undivided attention. Peter's question and undoubted impending summary of his latest case, had put pay to that. George put down the tiny gear wheels and leant back in his chair.

The Chief Inspector took another digestive from the plate next to his cup and saucer.

'Right, Peter, you have my full attention,' George said. 'And have consumed half a packet of my favourite digestive biscuits.'

'That's rich, coming from a man who emptied my entire drinks cabinet of single malt whiskey.'

'You only had one bottle.'

'Doesn't matter, you still emptied my entire drinks cabinet of single malt whiskey,' Peter exclaimed.

'And you drank half of it.'

'Irrelevant. Extraneous detail,' he said with a dismissive wave of his second biscuit. 'Anyway, back to the case that is taxing my brain at present.'

The Professor made no comment.

'Two nights ago, Margaret Knowles, aged sixty-three, was poisoned in her niece's third floor flat in Midsummer Common, Cambridge. The only other person in the flat was the said niece, Angela Galbraith, aged twenty-seven, incapacitated after a recent skiing accident.'

'Incapacitated, in what way?' the Professor asked.

'Broken left leg and dislocated right hip,' the Chief Inspector clarified. 'Her aunt, Margaret, was staying with her while she recovered. She needed assistance to get dressed/undressed, washing/showering, toilet and....oh you know, the usual female activities.' The Professor smiled. He was surprised for a long-serving police officer, Peter still got uncomfortable talking about *ladies' matters*.

'The emergency call was received at 20:53 saying an elderly lady was vomiting and extremely unwell. An ambulance was dispatched from Addenbrooke's - it arrived within fifteen minutes. When the paramedics got to the flat, Margaret was lying on the bathroom floor and had extreme difficulty in breathing – her heart beat was also erratic. They didn't delay. They fetched the trolley and rushed her back to the hospital. Margaret Knowles arrived in the A&E ward just after nine thirty. She died ten minutes later. The A&E doctor who attended her was very suspicious about her symptoms and telephoned the police.'

The Professor sat with his elbows on his desk, his chin resting on his clasped hands. Murders both upset and fascinated him.

'While Detective Sergeant Brookes was on his way Angela Galbraith and her parents, who also live in Cambridge, arrived at the hospital. Angela's mother, Eleanor was Margaret's sister.'

The Professor nodded.

'Margaret Knowles's body was taken straight to the pathology lab and aconitine and isoaconitine were identified in her body.'

'Aconite?' the Professor gasped.' Nasty, nasty stuff.'

Aconite or *Aconitum napellus,* to give it its correct horticultural name, is one of the most poisonous plants in the UK. It is referred to more frequently as monkshood, wolf's bane, leopard's bane, devil's helmet and blue rocket. It grows in garden and in the wild, displaying predominately blue - purple hooded flowers in late summer. The root and leaves contain various potent alkaloids such as aconitine, isoaconitine, lycaconitine and napelline.

It is obviously highly toxic if ingested, but it also has the ability to enter the body through the skin if the plant is touched accidently.

Rumour has it that the Roman Emperor Claudius was murdered with aconite and the plant has enjoyed a dark prominence throughout history as the *perfect poison* with the only post-mortem signs being asphyxia.

If poisoning occurs through picking the leaves, tingling will start at the point of absorption and extend up the arm to the shoulder, after which the heart will start to be affected.

If ingested, the initial signs are a sensation of burning, tingling, and numbness in the mouth and face, followed by nausea and vomiting, sweating, dizziness and difficulty in breathing. The main causes of death are failure of the respiratory system and the heart. There is no known antidote.

'How was it administered?'

'In her drink – Vodka and bitter lemon.'

'Unusual drink?' the Professor frowned.

'Well, she and Angela liked the flavour and used to have one most evenings.'

'Girls will be girls,' the Professor chuckled.

He rubbed his chin.

'No doubt poured out by Angela?'

'Hardly – it is a struggle for her to get out of her chair,' the Chief Inspector scowled. 'No, Margaret poured them out.'

'The plot thickens.'

'So, back to the hospital,' the Chief Inspector said. 'DS Brookes telephoned me and I drove down there.'

The Chief Inspector reached across and took a third digestive biscuit.

'Right, that's your quota,' George cried reaching across and removing the plate of biscuits from beside Peter's cup and saucer.

'The house-keeping a bit tight this month?' Peter joked.

'No, but you will finish them all before Dorothy can go shopping again.'

The two pals grinned at one another.

'So, Peter, you arrived at the hospital.'

'Oh yes. I spoke to the doctor in A&E and then the guy in the path. Lab who had confirmed aconite was present in Margaret's body. Finally, I went upstairs and met Angela and her parents – nice family. Angela Galbraith is a sweet, blonde-haired, young girl and an enchanting smile. Do you know George after thirty years a copper you develop a sixth sense for villains and killers - Angela Galbraith is not in that category.'

The Professor raised an eyebrow.

'She might be schizophrenic, have dual-personality or hear 'voices' – history is littered with them, Peter.'

'George, I *am* a copper. I do know those characteristics. I still say she doesn't fit the profile,' he glowered. 'Anyway, I questioned her and took her statement at the hospital. Finally, at nearly midnight, her parents took her back to their place.'

'You didn't arrest her?'

'Circumstantial evidence and disabled to boot. Fools rush in where angels fear to tread, George. Anyway, with her leg in plaster, she is hardly going anywhere.'

'But, she remains your prime suspect?'

'Has to be. She and her aunt were alone in the flat all day. Apparently, Margaret's son popped in during the morning. But yes, those two were alone in the flat all evening.'

'Margaret Knowles didn't take the poison herself or by accident?'

'A rather bizarre thing to do, 'the Chief Inspector said draining his cup of tea. 'If you want to top yourself, there are far quicker and less painful ways to do it.'

The Professor nodded.

'Any motive?' he asked.

'I have Roger going into the family history as we speak. Margaret Galbraith has a brother, Michael, as well as her sister, Eleanor. He has two children, so Roger is doing the circuit. As far as I can see Angela Galbraith has no motive. In fact, almost the reverse. While she is incapacitated, Margaret was her life-line – doing the shopping, cooking, washing and generally looking after her.'

'Cutting the branch off the tree whilst you are sitting on it.'

'Precisely.'

'So, no motive, and no poison bottle,' the Professor said staring at his friend. 'Only opportunity. Just one out of the categorical trinity.'

'Well, one and half. We know Margaret was poisoned, we just have no bottle.'

'Which neatly brings us back to the beginning of this conversation – where does one hide a poison bottle?' the Professor frowned.

He turned slowly in his chair and gazed out of the side window at his rear garden.

'To be honest Peter, if you are intending to poison someone, the last place you put the poison is in a small brown bottle with a skull and crossbones on the label and then place it in the bathroom cabinet.'

The Chief Inspector laughed.

'You hide it is an everyday container – an eye-drops bottle, a pill bottle, a plastic soap container. For that matter, any everyday household item - an empty tomato sauce bottle or an empty bottle of bleach – something that just doesn't attract attention,' the Professor said slowly turning back to face the Chief Inspector.

'We've done all that, George. SOCO have taken most of the contents of Angela's kitchen and bathroom down the lab.'

'And nothing?'

'Nothing.'

'Okay, Option Two. Temporarily hide it. Usually down the side of the chair cushion is a favourite. Or, tuck it in a discarded Kleenex tissue and place that in an empty crisp or peanuts bag then toss the pair into the wastepaper bin.'

'Checked all those.'

'Has the flat got a rubbish chute?'

'No, plastic bags. Checked those.'

'Has the flat got a waste-disposal unit?'

'No.'

The Professor let out a loud snort of disappointment.

'Option Three – conceal it before permanent disposal. Put it in your pocket, for ladies down their bra or in their underwear. I assume Angela didn't have a full body search?'

'What? Not from me at the hospital?' the Chief Inspector spluttered.

'Just asking,' the Professor grinned.

'Anyway, staying with that option, Angela could have left the flat with the bottle concealed somewhere about her person and between her flat and the hospital managed to get rid of it.'

'The waste bins at the hospital?'

'Bins by the flat, out of the car window as they drove along. The possibilities are endless, Peter.'

The Professor turned away and thought for a second.

'Of course, Margaret Knowles began to have a reaction to the poison well before the ambulance was called. Margaret would start by saying she felt unwell probably half an hour before collapsing on the floor. Angela had quite a bit of time to hobble to the window and throw the bottle out.'

'The flat has a large patio door which was open.'

'Well, there you are. Angela didn't even have to stir from her chair. She lobbed the bottle through the large opening. What's below?'

'The resident's garden.'

'Checked it?'

'With a fine-tooth comb.'

'Good lad,' the Professor smiled. 'Well, let's forget this last option. My money is on in the bra and out of the window en-route to Addenbrooke's.'

'I am glad you never decided to turn to crime, George. I would have had a devil of a job catching you.' the Chief Inspector laughed.

'If I am *that* good, what's to say I haven't?'

The Chief Inspector stared hard at his colleague for a few seconds. The Professor released a placating smile.

'Okay, I trust you,' Peter said slowly.

'So, back to Angela Galbraith, you want to find that poison bottle?'

Peter nodded.

'But, by your reckoning, George, there may not be any bottle to locate?'

'Just my assessment – I am not always right.'

'I will remember that line.,' the Chief Inspector grinned.

He screwed his face up.

'Only *opportunity* and half a *means*. I can't see a jury convicting on that - even assuming the Crown Prosecution would agree to proceed on this meagre basis. So, all our money is riding on Roger finding a motive,' he grimaced.

The Chief Inspector rose to his feet.

'I am going over to Angela's flat to meet Roger. Want to come over and see if you can spot something lesser mortals, like police officers, have missed?'

The Professor laughed.

'Now, how could I decline such a wonderful challenge.'

The Professor gazed longingly at his Victorian clock movement on his desk and raised an eyebrow.

'I shall return my lovelies and put you all back together,' he cried.

The Chief Inspector gave him a curious look.

'Do you always talk to your clocks?'

'Oh, yes, they are my little children.'

The Chief Inspector shook his head.

'I am so glad that I fish as a hobby.'

'Don't you talk to the fish when you are sitting on the bank?'

'Certainly not. Other fisherman would think I had gone round the twist.'

The Professor grabbed his trusty brown leather briefcase full of useful tools like screwdrivers. tweezers, magnifying glass, plastic bags, dusting powder and other little tools invaluable for forensic scenes.

'Just off with Peter,' the Professor called to his wife from the hallway.'

'Good,' Dorothy replied. 'Perhaps I can now get my car out of the garage and go shopping.'

'Oh, sorry, Dorothy, am I blocking you in?'

'Yes,' she retorted.

'And he's eaten most of the digestive biscuits,' George bellowed.

'I will get some more when I am out,' said Dorothy. 'Perhaps I will treat you to a packet of those chocolate covered ones.'

'Don't tell Peter, otherwise we'll never get rid of him.'

'Oooo, chocolate digestive biscuits,' Peter smiled.

'See, I told you,' George cried.

'Anyone would think it was your birthday.'

'Last week it was,' George snapped.

'Oh that's right, Rita bought you a card,' Peter remembered.

'And signed it from both of you.'

'Pressure of work, I haven't time to do everything myself,' Peter said dolefully.' Come on, George, Roger is waiting for us at Midsummer Common.'

The Chief Inspector turned and marched out the door.

'Won't be long,' the Professor said giving Dorothy a peck on the cheek.

'I have heard that more than once,' she responded with a broad grin. 'Six hours later………'

The Professor hurried across the drive to the passenger's side of the Chief Inspector's large BMW 520 with its gleaming anthracite paintwork.

'Oh, I get to sit in the front as you're driving,' the Professor smiled.

'Well don't make the carpets mucky.'

The Professor glanced down at his polished brown brogues.

'Bring my slippers next time,' he muttered.


It was a relatively short drive across Cambridge to the district of Midsummer Common – nestling between the world-famous Jesus College, the city and the River Cam. The traffic in the centre was going at its usual snail's pace which frustrated Peter. However, it gave George a chance to gaze out of the side window and marvel at the skyline and the incredible architecture of his city. He had seen it a thousand times, but it never failed to stir strong emotions of delight, pride and a sense of being a part of the great historical city.

'One-four-nine-two,' Peter muttered.

'What is?' the Professor asked as he turned back.

'The access code to the complex – they are prominent dates.'

'One-four-nine-two,' the Professor repeated. 'Oh, 1492, Columbus sailed the ocean blue.'

'They change the code every six-months,' Peter added.

'A simple and sensible measure.'

'Simple?' the Chief Inspector cried, 'They formed a sub-committee just to draw up the numbers.'

The Professor laughed.

'You're joking?'

'Certainly not. There was nearly a riot two years ago, Angela's father told Roger.'

'Over the access code?'

'The property management company who administered the access code at the time, had installed zero-zero-three-four.'

'0034 - what's prominent about that?'

'George, you are a heathen. That was the date that our dear Lord, Jesus Christ was crucified.'

'Oh, yes.'

'I can see that your days at Sunday School didn't do you a power of good,' the Chief Inspector grinned.

'Anyway, the non-Christian residents of the flats objected.'

'Really?'

'Serious business, this access code issue. So the property management company relented and opted for a more homespun number – 1666, the Great Fire of London.'

'Harmless enough,' the Professor shrugged.

'Oh, not so. Now, the Christian faction decided that was too close to the sign of the Devil.'

'What, 666? Ye gods.' George exclaimed.

'So, the residents said they would draw up their own list of acceptable access-codes which the property management company could use. So, lo and behold, the Marlborough Court Residents - Access Code Sub-Committee was formed.'

The Professor chuckled.

'1666 was duly removed,' the Chief Inspector continued, 'and 1918, the end of World War One was installed.'

'Armistice Day - clearly no German residents at Marlborough Court,' the Professor grinned.

'There it is, up ahead,' the Chief Inspector pointed through the windscreen.

The Professor focussed on a modern three storey block at the end of the road with an imposing brick and wrought-iron perimeter.

'L-shaped is it?' he asked as he peered through the windscreen.

'No, you can only see half of it from here. It is four-sided with a residents' private garden in the centre.'

'A square doughnut?'

'That's it.'

The Chief Inspector brought the car to a halt just in front of the wrought iron gates. Through the gates, they could see Sergeant Carter's car and a white SOCO (Scene of Crime Office) van parked in the "visitors" parking spaces directly ahead of them.

The Chief Inspector wound down his window and leaned towards the keypad set into the gate pillar. He keyed in "one-four-nine-two".

The unit returned a rude-sounding buzz.

The Chief Inspector stared at the gates, but they didn't move.

'Bloody technology,' he swore and keyed in the number again.

He received a second electronic 'raspberry' and still the gates didn't move.

The Chief Inspector dived into his pocket and pulled out his mobile phone.

'Roger, I am trying to get through the entrance gates –'

'- Ah, they have changed the number, sir' Sergeant Carter interrupted.

'Done what?' the Chief Inspector exclaimed.

'Changed the number. The residents thought because of the incident two nights ago that they should change the access code.'

'Roger, this is a bloody murder scene, the residents mustn't go round altering or changing anything,' the Chief Inspector exploded.

George sat there quietly – it was safer. Nevertheless, as a spectator, it was always amusing when Peter lost his cool and went into Rambo-mode.

'So what's the new code?' he barked.

'One-five-eight-eight, sir.'

'1588?' the Chief Inspector snapped, 'Prominent date, my ass. What on earth happened then?'

'The English defeated the Spanish Armada,' the Professor said in a soft unassuming tone. 'I deduce that there are no Spanish residents in Marlborough Court either.'

The gates finally swung open and the Chief Inspector accelerated angrily into the vacant parking space ahead of him.

As the two climbed out of the car, a rather flustered Roger came running round the corner of the building. The Professor assumed he was fearing a further lashing from Peter's tongue for allowing the access-code to be changed.

'Sorry about the access-code,' Roger called out as he hurried towards them.

'Always best to have the first word, especially an apology,' the Professor smiled.

'Have they touched anything else?' the Chief Inspector barked.

'No, sir.'

'Good,' the Chief Inspector grunted.

'Morning, Roger,' the Professor called, hoping to move the subject on.

'Morning, Professor,' he replied as he handed both gentlemen the requisite light blue plastic suits.

The Chief Inspector grunted again. He hated dressing up in these oversized condoms, as he called them.

The Professor studied the outside of the three-storey residential block. Evidently built in the last ten years judging by the design, the cleanliness of the bricks and the roof tiles. He noted two security cameras positioned halfway up the corners facing one another and the central entrance.

'Angela Galbraith's flat is in the right hand block. So, if we go in through this entrance,' Roger gestured.

'Lead on,' the Chief Inspector ordered.

As they turned the corner, a similar façade to the front came into sight.

'Oh, it is a giant brick square,' the Professor muttered.

'Like a square Polo mint.' Roger replied,

The Chief Inspector didn't comment.

The Professor looked up to see another pair of cameras fixed to the corners on the building.

'Quite a secure building,' he commented.

'Oh, yes,' Roger replied. 'The outside is covered by CCTV cameras, together with the four lobbies and each corridor.'

'Hmmmm,' the Professor reflected. 'You wouldn't expect any trouble in such a property.'

'They are rather exclusive,' Roger added, 'so the residents rather expect the best for their money.'

'How could Angela Galbraith afford to live here?' the Professor asked with a puzzled look on his face.

'She's a fashion model and entertainer,' Roger replied.

'You have done your homework,' the Chief Inspector said acerbically.

Roger nevertheless managed a smile.

'Well, I spent yesterday talking to her family, sir.'

'Am I likely to have seen her in a magazine or on television?' the Professor asked with renewed interest.

'Possibly,' Roger replied. 'But, she's not in the Kate Moss or Naomi Campbell class. And her entertainment field is really just a magician's assistant - like Debbie Magee was to the late Paul Daniels.'

'You are well-versed in fashion models and the like, Roger,' the Chief Inspector said dryly.

The Sergeant glanced at the Professor and raised an eyebrow.

The sergeant ran forward and entered the 1588 access code. The door buzzed and he pulled it open as the Chief Inspector and the Professor strode through.

The Professor stopped and surveyed the entrance lobby. It was clean and functional with a central lift door and a staircase to the left. He gazed up at the further security camera set high on the wall pointing at the entrance.

'The flat is on the third floor, shall we take the lift?' Roger enquired.

Before the Chief Inspector had a chance to even suggest walking, the Professor advocated the lift.

The lift doors opened on the third floor, to show a bright, carpeted corridor.

'Six doors down on the left,' Roger directed. 'Number 311.'

As they walked down the corridor, Roger continued his estate-agent patter.

'All the outside flats have magnificent views of the city, the colleges or the River Cam. In this West Wing, the flats on the right are the premier one, with views of the spires of Jesus College. Angela Galbraith's flat is on the other side. It has a wide balcony that looks down on the communal gardens. Not quite so breath-taking but still pleasant.'

The two detectives halted by her door as Roger removed the door key from his pocket.

The Professor overshot and walked on to the smoke detector screwed to the ceiling.

'Fire-drill is not on our agenda today, George,' the Chief Inspector called out.

'No, I was just checking. It is the sort that has an integral security camera in it, I believe.'

'Really?' the Chief Inspector replied. 'If the system was working on Tuesday, we must have miles of footage covering the whole building.' He glanced at Roger, who half-smiled. He was the poor soul who would have to go through all that.

The three donned their light-blue plastic overalls and entered the flat. An officer from SOCO was checking the list that he held in his hand as he replaced the items in the bathroom cabinet.

'Chief Inspector Meadows,' Peter called out.

The officer nodded

'I am nearly finished, sir. I will be out of your way in five minutes.'

The Professor stood arms folded and surveyed the flat. In front of him was the airy lounge stretching forward to the wide patio doors that opened out onto a balcony. Just before those doors was a doorway to the right. through which George could see a gas hob.

'Clearly the kitchen,' he deduced

As he stood at the top of the lounge, to his immediate right was the bathroom where the SOCO officer was working.

He took a couple of paces down the corridor outside of that bathroom until he glimpsed, through the open doorways, two bedrooms at the far end.

The Professor strolled back to where the two detective were standing.

'Nice place,' he commented.

'Commanding a premium price,' Roger said with his estate agent hat on again.

'This is the chair Angela Galbraith was sitting in on Tuesday,' the Chief Inspector said placing his hands on the back of the beige armchair.

'Margaret Knowles was in that one,' he pointed at the other identical armchair. 'Between them was a nest of tables on which the two glasses stood. Those two items are down the lab at present.'

'Well, Roger,' the Chief Inspector asked enthusiastically, 'have you found me a motive?'

Roger paused.

'Sorry, sir, no.'

That was not the answer Peter was hoping for and his face hardened.

'All done,' the SOCO officer called as he made his way to the main door.

'Thank you,' the Chief Inspector waved.

He turned back to his assistant.

'So no obvious motive?' the Chief Inspector grimaced.

'No, sir. I spoke to Angela's uncle, Michael, and his son and daughter,' Roger continued. 'Angela's an easy going girl and she doesn't appear to have had any ructions or falling out with any members of the family.'

The Chief Inspector glanced at the Professor. His frustrated look spoke volumes.

'The only recent disagreement in the family was between the deceased and her son, Paul Knowles,' Roger read from his notebook. 'He and his father, Timothy, spent years restoring an Austin Healey 3000. When his father died, two years ago, bearing in mind how much time and effort Paul had personally expended on the restoration, he assumed that the car would come to him. That provision was not made in his father's will. Paul Knowles demanded the car. His mother took umbrage and said no. Her son then became very abusive, threatening to take her to court over the matter. Margaret's brother said that if only Paul hadn't been so offensive and more reasonable, Margaret would have willingly given him the car. What did she want with an old sports car, anyway? A bitter feud developed between them and, on principle, she flatly refused to ever consider giving him the car – she would send it to the breaker's yard first.'

'Oh family feuds,' the Professor sighed. 'The problems and waste of energy they cause.'

'So Paul Knowles fell out with his mother. Does that help us in any way?' the Chief Inspector asked.

'Paul Knowles was at this flat Tuesday morning,' Roger said assertively.

'So he was.' Peter's eyes flashed. 'I had nearly forgotten that detail.'

'Why was he here?' the Professor asked Roger.

He looked at the Chief Inspector.

'It was late. I can't remember if she gave a reason.'

'But the angry son was here Tuesday morning,' said the Professor and rubbed his chin.

'Our killer, George?' the Chief Inspector suggested. 'And with a definite motive.'

'Hold on Judge Jefferies, before you string him up,' the Professor cried. 'Paul Knowles was here in the flat in the morning?'

'About ten thirty,' Roger said glancing at his notebook.

'Margaret Knowles was poisoned about eight o'clock that evening – ten hours later.'

'He spiked her drink,' the Chief Inspector said with gusto.

'How?' The Professor countered. 'Margaret poured out the drinks, you told me. I would assume she selected two clean glasses. You would hardly choose a glass with a murky white liquid in the bottom.'

'Paul Knowles spiked the vodka,' the Chief Inspector retaliated.

'Why didn't Angela die as well?'

'Oh.'

'I know,' Roger joined in. 'He made an ice cube of aconite.'

'Fifty-fifty chance who would get that,' said the Professor.

'Did they both have ice in their drinks?' Roger asked.

'I would assume so.'

'But we need to ask Angela that. It is a faint possibility if she *never* has ice in her drinks.' the Chief Inspector nodded.

'A highly risky approach. Not one a killer would chance – not unless he didn't care how many people he killed,' the Professor declared.

'Her uncle said Paul and Angela were very close,' Roger chipped in.

'Well, that shoots a hole in that theory,' the Professor said folding his arms.

'I assume that Angela and Margaret didn't have different dinners?' he asked.

'No, the same lasagne, if I remember correctly,' the Chief Inspector replied, glancing at Roger who nodded.

The Chief Inspector caught the thrust of the Professor's question.

'Oh, right. From the forensic report, aconite was only found in Margaret Knowles's glass, nowhere else in the flat.'

The Professor stared hard at the two detectives.

'I can't see any way that Paul Knowles could have set up the poisoning of his mother ten hours previously and ensure Angela was not harmed.'

He shook his head.

'Motive, but no means.'

He walked down to the kitchen – a bright, sparkling provision with clean, white appliances. He gave it a cursory inspection.

'SOCO have crawled all over this lot,' he muttered.

'Can I?' he asked as he wandered over to the patio doors.

'Be our guest,' the Chief Inspector gestured.

The Professor slid open the large doors and stepped out onto the balcony.

He surveyed the quadrangle. On three sides were an array of flats all facing onto the private, central garden which was mainly laid to lawn other than the two large bushes in diagonal corners, complemented by a vibrant, multi-coloured flower bed in each of the other corners.

His eyes hopped from flat to flat. Many had large colourful pots and planters on their balconies – an attractive means of bringing a little bit of the natural world into an apartment lifestyle. An assortment of decorative sun chairs and recliners were on display on many balconies. Small patio dining tables and chairs were also evident. Beside a couple stood tall gas heaters erect like small lamp posts - clearly allowing dining to continue even if there was a chill in the air. The large patio doors of many apartments were dressed with gleaming white vertical blinds to shield the occupants from the afternoon sun and provide a high degree of privacy. It was obvious that this was comfortable, affluent living within a stone's throw of the centre of Cambridge.

'Very attractive,' he commented.

His eyes scanned the flats opposite.

'Almost the perfect neighbourhood watch too,' he smiled.

The other two joined the Professor on the balcony.

'Have we interviewed any of the residents opposite?' the Professor asked.

'This afternoon's job,' Peter replied looking at his sergeant.

'Just in case anyone saw anything suspicious. A lovely warm spring evening, many could be out on their balconies.' the Professor added.

He glanced back into the lounge.

'I suppose if it hadn't been for Angela Galbraith's disability, she and Margaret might have sat out here themselves on that fateful night.'

'Possibly', the Chief Inspector replied. 'They had the patio doors wide open to let in fresh air, though.'

The Professor wandered back and stood in the middle of the lounge. His eyes travelled through three-hundred and sixty degrees.

'Your thoughts, George,' Peter said as he walked up to join him.

'It is small, neat and tidy. It isn't like a rambling mansion with rooms all over the place and half an acre of stables.'

'Bijou, the estate agents call it. Anything you want to pull apart?'

The Professor glanced around again.

'I am sure the SOCO team have looked in all the right places – they know what they are doing.'

'They haven't taken the carpets up yet.'

'I don't think there is any need for that, Peter. I don't think the poison bottle, or whatever container it was in, is still in this flat.'

The Professor chose not to sit in either of the armchairs, but pulled out one of the dining table chairs. The Chief Inspector pulled out another. Roger decided it was appropriate to stand.

'Peter, I don't think you are going to find that bottle.'

'You don't think so?'

The Chief Inspector looked up with a disappointed expression.

'Forget that approach. You have half of the *means*. Margaret Knowles was poisoned – that is a fact. Someone administered that. Angela Galbraith was with her all evening and they had no visitors – circumstantial, but good enough in my book.'

The Chief Inspector looked a tad happier.

'Forgive me, Peter, I think you have more than half of the *means*. I think you have nearly the whole element.'

'You think so?'

'I do.'

'So, let's move on. Let's try and build up the rest of the evidence from another direction.'

He paused and glanced towards the patio doors.

'Peter, this building is bristling with security cameras, I have never seen so many. Let's see if that gives us a clue as to the comings and goings to this flat on Tuesday. We know Paul Knowles is one, There may be others.........'

He paused again and an almost painful expression ran across his face.

'Time,' he cried.

The Chief Inspector looked at his wristwatch.

'No, not *the* time. The amount of time Angela had.'

Peter shook his head - he still hadn't latched onto George's drift.

'I could kick myself, Peter, I said it earlier. Margaret Knowles probably began feeling unwell at least half an hour before the ambulance arrived. The last ten minutes she would be vomiting and writhing in agony. There is no way she would be aware of what was going on in the lounge. Even if she were, Angela knew that Margaret would never tell - she would take any observations with her to the grave.

I talked about throwing the bottle out of the patio door during this period. That proposal we have discounted. But it still doesn't remove the fact that Angela had a very lengthy period of time to remove the bottle from the flat.'

'She hobbled downstairs to the waste-bin?' Peter suggested.

'Probably a shade risky. If she bumped into any of her neighbours, her pretence of attending to her aunt while she awaited the ambulance, would go straight out the window.'

The Professor rubbed his chin.

'No, it is a bit of a mystery.'

'One of your famous locked room mysteries?' Roger smiled.

The Professor looked around at the room.

'I guess it is. It is a flat on the third floor, no one came in or out during the fateful evening.

The only difference is, besides the victim, a second person shared the ill-fated room. I guess we could call it a locked room murder-plus-one mystery,' he chortled. 'But all indicators point to that one being the killer. But the murder weapon?...or in this case a bottle....'

The Professor paused again. A wry smile ran across his face.

'Hold on....I have just had a brainwave.'

'Oh, I wish I had as many as you do, George,' the Chief Inspector grinned.

'Angela had plenty of time...I keep saying it,' he muttered as he screwed his face up and pondered the circumstances.

'What if she telephoned someone? Let's say, the angry son, Paul Knowles, who was waiting in his car parked outside in the car park – or better still, across the road.... Yes, I like it.' The Professor beamed. 'Paul hurries over, up the stairs and rings the doorbell. Angela hobbles to the door, opens it and hands him the bottle. As I just said, it makes no difference if his mother sees him, she will be dead shortly. With bottle in hand, or hidden in his coat pocket, he casually leaves the building.  A half an hour's drive towards Peterborough and you are in the bleak, watery-depth of the Fenland. Hide a single poison bottle up there? You could practically hide the year's output from United Glass up there and nobody would notice.'

'George, you have an amazing imagination,' the Chief Inspector said.

'Too imaginative?'

'No, quite the reverse - I like it,' the Chief Inspector cried.

The Professor smiled.

'I am pleased. Now, Peter, you have a case that stands up. You have the *motive* from Paul Knowles and the *opportunity* and *means* from Angela Galbraith – the categorical trinity.'

'Do you remember I said ten minutes ago,' Roger chipped in, 'that their uncle said that Angela and Paul were quite close.'

'Right from the beginning, the cornerstone of this case has been the disposal of the poison bottle,' George reminded everyone.

'But more than that, George,' the Chief Inspector interjected. 'The disposal of the bottle has demonstrated to us that Angela had an accomplice – that is a valuable development.'

'Someone came to the door whilst Margaret was writhing in agony,' grimaced Roger.

'Who that person was, is still to be decided. Let's call him "The Man in the Corridor". But he completes the deadly alliance,' the Professor declared.

He smiled. The theory stacks up.

'It's funny Peter, the feature of a missing poison bottle which started as an annoyance and frustration has ended up a godsend.'

'Good work, George.' The Chief Inspector applauded.

He turned to Roger.

'No better time than the present. I want you to go through the CCTV footage of this whole building and document Paul Knowles's time and departure in the morning. Look out for any objects that he was carrying, including any suspicious bulges in his jacket or coat, or if he was holding his arms awkwardly. Then, go through all the footage between six o'clock Tuesday evening up to when Angela and her family departed for the hospital and see if anyone came to this flat or this floor.'

Roger nodded and headed for the door.

'Roger, when you've finished that, can you do some door-knocking on the residents in the flats opposite. I want to know if anyone saw anything suspicious on Tuesday evening....or for that matter, if they saw anything at all happening in this flat. There must be some nosey residents out there.'

The Chief Inspector turned back to his colleague.

'Do you think we've cracked it?' he asked.

The Professor gave a polite half-smile.

'No, Peter. It is just a theory. A theory where all the pieces fit. We need some more evidence before you crack open the bottle of champagne.'

'So where next, George?'

'Obviously, I want to speak with Angela Galbraith.'

'It is surprising if she finally turns out to be the killer,' the Chief Inspector said with a sombre look on his face. 'She really is a very sweet girl.'

'Let me be the judge of that,' the Professor cautioned.

'To kill her own aunt,' Peter said shaking his head in dismay.

'Margaret was Angela's mother's sister?'

'That's right.'

'Matertericide.'

'What is?'

'The killing of your maternal aunt.'

'You just made that up....didn't you?'

'Look it up when you get home,' the Professor smiled.

While Roger began the monumental task of locating and viewing the building's security tapes. The Chief Inspector and the Professor headed south across the city.

'Where are we heading?' the Professor asked.

'Bentley Road.'

'Where's that?'

'Off the Trumptington Road, opposite the lakes and golf course.'

'When we get in there, George, you do most of the talking and I will listen,' the Chief Inspector proposed. 'I know a large part of the story from Angela's statement at the hospital. Hopefully, with the two of us there, one of us will spot that chink in her armour.'

'Righto.'

After ten minutes, the Chief Inspector's BMW turned into a rather salubrious avenue of mainly mature detached houses.

'Oh, this is rather pleasant,' the Professor said looking attentively out of the side window. 'Do you know, Peter, I have lived in Cambridge for over twenty years and yet I have never been down this road before.'

'It isn't a through-road. It only feeds the adjoining three or four roads.'

'And Angela's parents live here?'

'Yes. He's a Consultant or a Registrar at Addenbrooke's, so I understand.'

The Professor gazed at the impressive mansion on his left.

'Clearly, they earn a lot more than humble lecturers,' he complained.

'And they earn more than policemen,' the Chief Inspector barked.

The Chief Inspector pulled onto the wide paved drive behind the white Range Rover Evoque.

It was a tall, slender man with neat grey hair, dressed in a navy lambswool jumper over grey trousers who answered the door.

'Good morning, Mr Galbraith. Chief Inspector Meadows, we met briefly at the hospital the other night.'

'Oh yes,' he half-smiled.

'This is my colleague Professor George Wellbelove.'

The two shook hands.

'I wonder if we can have a brief word with your daughter?'

'Well, she is upstairs resting. She is very upset.'

'I understand.'

'Who is it, Rex?' a lady's voice called out.

'The police, Eleanor.'

There was a muted curse from Eleanor and without further ado, a middle aged lady joined her husband at the front door.

'Good morning, Mrs Galbraith,' the Chief Inspector said.

'They want to talk to Angela,' Rex Galbraith grumbled.

'Well, she is still sobbing her heart out in her bedroom,' Eleanor Galbraith protested. 'Her aunt's death has come as a great shock to her. But to have the finger pointed at her as well, is too much for a young girl.'

'I don't need to stress that this is a serious crime and Angela is the only person who can throw any light on it,' the Chief Inspector said firmly. 'It is not just guilt I am trying to establish, it is innocence as well.'

Eleanor Galbraith looked at her husband,

'Well, I will go and get her.'

As she walked away, she stopped and turned to the Chief Inspector.

'She is not well. So for only a few minutes, and please be thoughtful and gentle with her.'

The Chief Inspector nodded.

As Mrs Galbraith headed up the large staircase, the Professor and the Chief Inspector followed Mr Galbraith into the lounge.

It was a generously proportioned room with two large floral print sofas and three matching armchairs – a pleasant blend of traditional with modern.

The Professor looked around the room but failed to see the customary and dominant television.

'Either concealed or they have an additional television lounge,' he mused.

The Professor and the Chief Inspector seated themselves on one of the sofas and Rex Galbraith sat like a king on his throne in one of the large armchairs. The three sat in silence, Rex staring disapprovingly at the visitors with his icy-blue eyes.

'My daughter has taken the death of her aunt rather badly,' he finally said sternly to remind his visitors.

'I do understand,' the Chief Inspector replied.

Rex grunted.

Silence descended on the lounge again as they awaited the arrival of Angela and her mother. The Professor was beginning to feel like the naughty schoolboy sent to the headmaster's office.

The Chief Inspector reached into his jacket pocket and retrieved Angela's formal statement. He unfolded and smoothed it out on the tops of his trouser legs and began reading.

The Professor reached into his jacket pocket – it was empty. He remembered that Dorothy had just brought it back from the dry-cleaners. His fingertips found their ticket attached to the jacket lining by a safety pin. He resisted taking that out and reading it. He folded his hands in his lap. He released a smile at Rex Galbraith, but it found no favour. He looked away and glanced around the room – he still couldn't see any television.

Eventually, Angela supported by her mother hobbled into the lounge. All three men rose. Rex hurried across the lounge and helped Angela into the other armchair.

The Professor studied the beautiful young girl. Admittedly she wore minimal makeup and her eyes were red from crying, but he could see how attractive she was. She had long honey blond hair reaching below her shoulders. Although it was spring, she wore a maroon tracksuit and the Professor could tell by the way it laid, she had indeed a very slender form.

She was clearly in discomfort as she shuffled in the seat. Finally, she managed to get herself comfortable. Her father pushed a footstool under her left leg. As she raised her leg, the Professor glimpsed the white plaster of the cast.

'Incapacitated is certainly the right word for her predicament,' he thought.

Her mother perched on the arm of the chair.

Angela thanked her father and finally looked up at the two visitors with her attractive icy-blue eyes.

'Morning,' she smiled. 'I understand you want to talk to me?'

'Miss Galbraith, I have brought along my colleague, Professor George Wellbelove who is a renowned specialist in forensic science to help me to get to the bottom of this baffling case.'

Angela nodded.

'Morning,' the Professor said softly.

'Miss Galbraith, we have your statement that I took at the hospital on Tuesday evening, but there are a few more questions we need to ask you,' the Chief Inspector began.

Her eyes filled with concern.

'I didn't kill my aunt,' she cried out.

There was real pain and anguish written across her face.

'No, no dear, of course you didn't,' her mother said putting her arm around her daughter's shoulders.

'I swear it. Why would I want to harm her? I loved my aunt.' And she burst into tears.

Rex rose from his chair and he and Eleanor comforted their sobbing daughter.

The Professor began to feel quite uncomfortable. He stared at the lovely young girl in so much distress. He glanced sideways.

The Chief Inspector sat motionless and impassively staring at Angela.

'I imagine he has had to deal with this situation far more times than I have had to,' he thought to himself.

The Professor's eyes wandered from person to person. Rex Galbraith looked very stern and Eleanor Galbraith stared daggers at the Chief Inspector.

Finally, Angela looked up with swollen tearful eyes.

'I am sorry.'

'Take your time,' the Chief Inspector said softly.

Angela Galbraith stopped mopping her eyes and pushed the white handkerchief up her tracksuit sleeve.

'I really loved my aunt,' she said. 'her death has really upset me.'

'Please don't apologise, Miss Galbraith,' the Chief Inspector said gently. 'I am sorry to cause you so much upset, but we have to get to the bottom of the circumstances surrounding your aunt's death. You may be the only person who can provide that information.'

The Professor glanced sideways. Peter's comment was well-chosen. George was pleased that Peter had used the term *death* rather than *murder*.

Rex Galbraith returned to his armchair.

The Chief Inspector cleared his throat.

'I am sorry to make you re-live the events of last Tuesday, but to help me and the Professor, I would like you to take us through the day again.'

Angela nodded.

'Before we do that, can I ask one question?'

Angela nodded again.

'Miss Galbraith do you know what aconite is?'

Rex Galbraith went to speak, but the Chief Inspector raised his hand to stop him.

'It is most important that your daughter answers all of our questions without your intervention,' the Chief Inspector said firmly.

Rex Galbraith sunk back into his armchair.

Angela Galbraith hesitated and pondered the question. She looked from one parent to another.

'Aconite? Is it the material they make those lovely black shiny worktops out of?'

The Professor smiled and glanced at the Chief Inspector, who scribbled something on the piece of paper that he was holding.

'Is that right? Probably not. I think I am muddling it up with granite. So what is it?' she asked.

The Chief Inspector shook his head as he wrote.

'No nothing to do with worktops,' the Professor interjected. 'We will come back to it in a moment.'

Angela smiled.

'Right,' the Professor began, 'as the Chief Inspector said, can we return to last Tuesday. Your aunt and you have had breakfast. What happened next?'

'I read the newspaper and my aunt her book.'

'Nothing else until approximately ten thirty?'

'Why ten thirty?'

'At that time you received the day's first visitor - Mr Paul Knowles, your cousin and your aunt's son?'

'That's correct,' Angela replied. 'In fact, our only visitor that day... oh, hold on, there was the meter-man who came about two o'clock to read the gas and electricity meters.'

'We're jumping ahead, but let's clear this guy as he has been mentioned. He arrived after lunch to read the meters'

'That's right.'

'Where are they situated?' the Professor asked.

'In the airing-cupboard, just outside of my bedroom,' she stated. 'Oh, you don't know where that is?'

'Yes I do, we have just visited the flat,' the Professor replied.

Angela looked a little uncomfortable with that news – her precious apartment – violated. But she had to accept that her lovely flat was now no longer home, but a crime-scene.

'Okay, so let's return to the morning. You agree that Paul Knowles arrived at ten thirty. Is that accurate?'

'Yes, Paul arrived a few minutes after half past ten. Say, ten thirty-five or six,' she said wrinkling her nose.

'The purpose of his visit?'

'To give me a pair of beautiful earrings.'

'It wasn't your birthday?'

'No,' she smiled. 'Let me explain. Paul and I both have birthdays in August – the 8th and 12th. Our birthstone is the green peridot.'

The Professor nodded.

'I had a lovely pair that my grandmother gave me.' She glanced at her mother who smiled.

'I used to wear them a lot, but somehow, I lost one. I was devastated. Paul, the clever thing that he is, found a pair in a jeweller in Cambridge and bought them for me. He is such a sweetie.'

'So, he called in briefly just after ten thirty to give you the earrings?' the Professor summarised. 'Did he talk to his mother?'

Angela frowned.

'They don't speak. There was a huge falling-out over a car that he and his father restored. Paul and I sat down in the lounge and Auntie Margaret went and read a book in her bedroom.'

'What was Paul wearing? The Chief Inspector interjected.

Angela frowned.

'It was warm so I think he just had a shirt and trousers – no jacket.'

He scribbled a note on his piece of paper.

'Apart from your present, did Paul carry anything else?' the Professor asked.

'Such as what?' Angela said with a puzzled expression of her face.

'A bottle,' the Chief Inspector interjected.

'A bottle of what?' she exclaimed and then the penny dropped. 'You are not suggesting that he poisoned his own mother? He's not like that. He's a real sweetie. They might be having a row over that blessed car, but that argument would have eventually blown over.'

She looked furiously from her mother to her father.

'Chief Inspector is that sort of insinuation necessary?' Rex Galbraith asked.

'Somehow poison entered Miss Galbraith's flat. If she didn't bring it, someone did.'

The three looked at one another – there was a profound logic in what the Chief Inspector had just said.

'Did Paul remain in the lounge?' the Professor resumed. 'For instance did he go to the toilet?'

'No, he was with me all the time,' Angela stated,' Oh, he did make us a cup of coffee. We chatted through the kitchen doorway.'

'How many cupboards did Paul have to go in to make the coffee?' the Chief Inspector asked.

'One for the two mugs. Everything else was on the work surface.'

He was in view all the time he was in the kitchen?'

'Yes,' Angela shouted.

'Sorry, I have to ask in order to get a comprehensive account of Tuesday,' the Chief Inspector stated.

He turned to the Professor to continue.

'And Paul left what time, Miss Galbraith?'

'About quarter past eleven.'

'Margaret Knowles came back into the lounge and we chatted. What happened next?' the Professor asked.

'We had lunch about one-ish.'

'Who made that?'

'Auntie Margaret. We had a round of tuna and cucumber sandwiches each and two individual bags of crisps.'

'To drink?'

'Auntie Margaret made us a cup of tea.'

The Professor glanced across at the Chief Inspector who was studying her statement.

'What did the two of you do all afternoon?' the Professor asked.

'Auntie Margaret read, I had a short doze, we chatted on and off and Aunty prepared the supper.'

'Apart from the meter man, no further visitors?'

'No.'

'So you didn't leave your seat all afternoon?'

'Well, once to go to the loo,' she said with a degree of embarrassment.

'I don't mean this to be a personal or embarrassing question, but did you go there all on your own or did your Aunt help you?' The Professor swallowed after asking the question.

'I do hope that is the only question you are going to ask on that sort of topic, Professor?' Eleanor Galbraith snapped.

'I purely wanted to establish whether Miss Galbraith made the journey on her own or whether your sister assisted her.'

Mrs Galbraith raised her eyebrows

'My Auntie used to help me. She said it took forever otherwise.'

She glanced at her mother who looked rather uncomfortable with the topic of toilets in general.

'To save you asking, Auntie Margaret would help me to unbutton my jeans, pull everything down and then retire to her bedroom.'

'Angela,' her mother exclaimed.

'Well, that sort of detail may help the gentlemen in this case.'

'Right, moving on,' the Professor said as he cleared his throat. 'The two of you next had supper. At what time?'

'About half past six. We both sat at the dining table.'

'What was served?'

'Lasagne and salad.'

'Prepared by whom?'

'Auntie Margaret.'

'In one large dish or two separate containers?'

'My large white ovenproof dish.'

The Chief Inspector was scribbling furiously.

'You finished supper at what time?' the Professor asked.

'About quarter past seven. Aunty Margaret cleared away, putting everything in the dishwasher. She then prepared two drinks.......'

She paused as the thoughts of the significance of that welled up inside her.

'Sorry,' she apologised.

'Take your time,' the Professor said softly.

'We both liked Vodka and bitter lemon. Auntie Margaret poured out two.'

'Two crystal glasses out of the wall cupboard in the kitchen?'

Angela nodded.

'Vodka bottle was where?'

'On the work surface.'

'Bitter lemon?'

'In a bottle in the fridge door.'

'Any ice in either them?'

The Professor sensed Peter looking up at that question.

'Yes, in both, I think.'

'You have ice in your drinks, Miss Galbraith?' the Chief Inspector interjected.

'Usually.'

Peter nodded, His eyes dulled-over– another theory down the pan.

'What happened next?' the Professor continued.

'Auntie Margaret turned on the television. We are both *Coronation Street* fans.' she smiled. 'Oh just for completeness, I went to the toilet again.'

Eleanor Galbraith let out a soft groan.

'Thank you,' the Professor raised his hand in apology, 'It is very useful to get a comprehensive picture of all events during the afternoon and evening. Continue, please.'

'Well, we sat and watched our programme. Oh, I missed out a part, Auntie Margaret went into her bedroom and got her glasses in order to watch the television.'

'How long was she gone?'

'About a minute.'

'Auntie Margaret was quite thirsty and finished her drink quite quickly – I sense she wanted to have a second one. I still had half of mine.'

Angela paused.

'You are sure the poison she took, was in her drink?'

'There is no other traces of aconite in the flat other than that in your Aunt's glass,' the Chief Inspector stated.

'Aconite,' Angela repeated. 'So that is what it is...the poison that killed.......' Her voice trailed away.

She stared hard at the Professor.

'Does that confirm my innocence in that I had never heard of this poison.....aconite?'

The Chief Inspector replied to the question.

'It is something we will take into account.'

'How did it get into Auntie's glass,' she asked without thinking.

'That is what we are attempting to find out,' the Professor replied.

He stared hard at her. He couldn't decide if she was an innocent victim or a very accomplished actress. Time would tell.

'Coming back to Tuesday evening, now about eight o'clock. How long after sipping her drink did your Aunt complain of any problems?'

'After about quarter of an hour. She complained that her throat was burning. She went and got a glass of water and sipped it. But within minutes she said it felt like her whole mouth was on fire. She thought that she was going down with a severe case of flu. She felt very cold. She then complained of tingling fingers and toes. "Oh I do feel unwell," she said. "If you don't mind, I will take myself off to bed. Hopefully this will pass and I will feel better in the morning."

She went off to bed and I remained in the lounge. About half an hour, maybe a shade later, I heard her get up and hurry to the bathroom to be sick. She called out to me. I struggled to my feet and got to her. I found her lying on the bathroom floor. She said her chest hurt and she was having trouble breathing. She asked me to phone for an ambulance. I shuffled along the floor to the telephone and dialled 999.'

'The emergency call was logged at 20:53,' the Chief Inspector said after referring to his notes. 'The ambulance arrived at 21: 10.'

Angela nodded.

'After making the emergency call, I telephoned my parents and told them that Auntie Margaret had become seriously unwell and that I had just called for an ambulance. They arrived at the flat at about....'

She looked to her father.

'We arrived at about quarter past nine, Margaret was on the trolley and the paramedics were about to take her down to the ambulance.'

'Thank you,' the Professor acknowledged and he turned back to Angela.

'My parents got me changed, locked up the flat and we headed for the hospital.'

The Professor turned and looked at the Chief Inspector. He cleared his throat.

'Thank you for that account, Miss Galbraith.'

She nodded.

'Can we leave that dreadful Tuesday and talk of other matters. I am happy if Mr and Mrs Galbraith would like to answer any of these questions. Did Margaret Knowles have any enemies you knew of?' the Chief Inspector asked.

'She fell out with her son Paul over this precious car he helped his father restore,' Eleanor Galbraith said strongly. 'Ungrateful bastard.'

'Paul is not that bad,' Angela said, springing to his defence.

'Let's not debate who is right and who is wrong. Can I just ask who started the feud?'

'He did,' Eleanor said emphatically.' My sister would have given him the blessed car if only he hadn't been so belligerent and obnoxious.'

The Chief Inspector glanced down and scribbled another note. He looked up.

'Other than her son, is there any other person she crossed swords with recently?' the Chief Inspector asked.

Eleanor shook her head.

'We are a pretty easy-going family.'

The Professor glanced at Rex Galbraith who had a bemused look on his face – perhaps he didn't agree.

'Any tradesmen or neighbours that Margaret Knowles had a run in with?' the Chief Inspector prompted.

'She didn't like Dave, my boyfriend,' Angela volunteered. 'He was a bit rough round the edges, but he was useful.'

'In what way?' the Professor asked.

'Well, it is a long story,' she began. 'I met Dave, Dave Saunders, at a club in Cambridge. He was good looking and amusing. We went out once, but he was not really my sort – a bit too macho. However, during our evening out, he said that he was a plumber.'

"That's interesting,' I said. 'I have a square loo that is a pain in the bum, literally."

'The flats at Marlborough Court are very well-designed, but the toilet features all have that designer look – aesthetically-pleasing, but not always practical. This square loo had driven me mad since I moved in. Well, Dave said he could change it. The only condition was he had to inspect my bum to get the right shape. You know the ploys men use to get you into bed, Chief Inspector?'

'Yes,' he replied in a rather awkward manner.

'Angela, is all this smutty-talk really necessary?' her mother snapped.

'I need to set the scene to explain, Dave's hatred of Auntie Margaret.'

Eleanor Galbraith shrugged her shoulders, but wasn't convinced.

'Well, I went out with him for a couple of weeks while he selected the most appropriate shape toilet and basin. I had already decided that after he had fitted the toilet and basin, he was history. He fitted them the week before I went off on my skiing holiday. Of course, when I finally returned to the flat, I was in plaster and accompanied by Auntie Margaret. Dave wanted to continue our relationship, but I wanted to end it. Plus, having Auntie Margaret staying made things very different. It was hard to find a way of having a private word with him – the flat's not that large. Anyway, Dave became an instant pain in the ass.'

Her mother flinched.

The Professor glanced over at her father who didn't seem to share his wife's Victorian view of human nature.

'Dave kept turning up at the flat expecting to get his leg over.'

Eleanor Galbraith choked and had a brief spell of coughing.

'Excuse me while I get a glass of water,' she said hurrying from the room.

" It's because that old girl is here," Dave shouted. But I told him that with my leg in plaster and my hip dislocated that *kitty was off limits*.'

Rex smiled – it was a good thing his wife was in the kitchen.

'Anyway, he stormed off. Which was just what I had wanted anyway.'

She looked at the Chief Inspector whose eyes were glazing over, but still following the story.

'I sense that Dave blamed Auntie Margaret for his sexual frustration, but really it was me. I had had enough of him. But at least I had my new loo,' she smiled.

Eleanor and glass of water returned to the lounge.

The Professor could sense that she wanted to ask "Have I missed anything?" but thank goodness, she resisted.

'Have you a mobile number for Mr Saunders?' the Chief Inspector asked.

'Yes,' Angela said rummaging in her tracksuit pocket for her phone. Her father picked up a small notebook and pen as he strode across the lounge towards her.

'Thank you,' she said and started scribbling.

She tore out the page and handed it to her father. Rex handed the slip of paper to the Chief Inspector as he returned to his seat.

'Thank you,' Peter said as he placed the slip in his inside jacket pocket.

The Professor sensed an air of devilment in Angela's eyes as she launched into a further episode of her relationships before Peter had a chance to change the subject.

'Before Dave was a hunky Australian business man over in this country for six months – Ben Masters. He was charming. He left London last autumn and returned to Sydney.... and his wife.'

Eleanor Galbraith coughed and took a large gulp of water.

Before the Chief Inspector could interrupt, Angela moved on to the next gentleman.

'Before Ben was Greg Willis, alias Greg Rocco, the magician. I went out with him for three months last year.'

'Oh he was nice,' her mother piped up. Angela's exploits seemed to be back in favour with her mother. 'He used to send her red roses every week.'

'He wanted me to be his stage assistant. We dated for a while, but I thought he was a creep.'

'But he is in showbiz and drives a Bentley Continental,' Eleanor added with a snooty smile.

'It is an old one,' Angela retorted.

'But still a Bentley, dear,' said Eleanor.

Angela shook her head.

'He has a flat in the East Wing of this building. That is when he is not touring.'

'He had a dove fly across and deliver a rose on her birthday. Isn't that romantic, Chief Inspector?' Eleanor added before Angela left the topic.

Peter was only half paying attention – the bubble had burst. He was beginning to get rather bored with the diary of a young Cambridgeshire girl.

'Even after we broke up he still sent me flowers to entice me into his act, as his stage assistant,' Angela snarled. 'Such a creep.'

'He still sends her white roses every month.'

'Mother,' Angela exclaimed, 'that's stopped, now I have signed a contract with Tony Warlock.'

'Who's Tony Warlock?' the Professor enquired.

'A better magician,' Angela snapped, 'who has been on the television. Although, after this skiing accident, I don't know if he will still want to employ me,' she gulped.

'Thank you, Miss Galbraith,' the Chief Inspector finally uttered, to halt any further exposés. 'We seem to have wandered off the original subject. The question I had asked was about

Margaret Knowles's enemies. From what you have just said they might include her son and Dave Saunders, the plumber.'

'Oh, not Paul, he is a sweetie. They were just having a family tiff,' Angela said jumping to his defence again.

The Chief Inspector ignored the comment.

'Are there any further people that we need to include? Please think, this may be important.'

Angela shook her head.

'Our neighbours liked Margaret.'

The Professor sat forward in his seat.

'Margaret Knowles was a widower,' His eyes travelled toward Eleanor, her sister. 'Did she ever mention or contemplate getting re-married?'

'Oh no, I don't think so.'

'What about companionship?' the Professor added.

'No, I don't think so,' Eleanor repeated.

'It is just if she had entered the world of Internet dating, there are a lot of genuine, single people, but because of the anonymity of the Internet, it can be a dark hiding-place for deceitful married men and predators.'

'Oh no, that is not Margaret's scene.'

'Thank you,' the Professor concluded, 'I just needed to ask.'

He turned and looked at the Chief Inspector.

'Mr Galbraith, I have to ask this. As a medical man, have you ever discussed poisons as a topic with your family?'

Rex Galbraith drew back.

'Rarely do I talk about my work at home, Chief Inspector. There is a thing called patient confidentiality. Plus, it isn't a subject my wife particularly enjoys talking about.'

The Chief Inspector glanced at Eleanor who nodded.

'I assume you have a few medical books at home, Mr Galbraith?'

'Three bookcases full of them,' his wife cried.' They are a pain to dust...so Maria, our cleaner, says.'

'Within these books are there reference books about poisons?'

Angela recoiled.

'Chief Inspector,' Rex Galbraith said sitting up straight. 'Any Tom, Dick or Harry can go onto the Internet and type the word "aconite" into Google and get all the information they need. They don't need my professional books.'

'I have never ventured into daddy's study, unless he was in there, anyway,' Angela protested.

The Chief Inspector looked from one to the other.

'Thank you, Mr Galbraith. Please forgive the question, but we must not overlook the fact that this is a murder investigation. I have to ask all sorts of unpleasant questions to track down the killer.'

Silence descended on the room. Angela went white. It was the first time that the words *murder* and *killer* had been said.

The Chief Inspector glanced down at his papers.

'I have Paul Knowles's home address, but can you tell me where he works?'

'Down at Crombie Nursery on the road to Royston,' Rex Galbraith pointed across the room in a southerly direction.

'Thank you.'

The Chief Inspector looked to his colleague.

'Any more questions, George?'

The Professor shook his head.

That was a cue for all, but Angela, to rise to their feet.

After the pleasantries, the Chief Inspector and the Chief Inspector departed and walked back to their car.

'Next stop, Crombie Nursery,' the Chief Inspector said as the he car turned out of the Galbraith's driveway.

'What are your thoughts, George?'

The Professor sighed.

'Angela Galbraith is a complicated person. She is young and part of this vibrant twenty-first century, but there is something multifaceted about her.'

'A murderess?'

'Let me sleep on that, Peter.'

'Right, let's go and see the non-Prodigal Son.'

As they headed down the Royston road the Professor looked out of the side window and pondered the conversation of the past half an hour.

'Something doesn't stack up,' he mused.

Within quarter of an hour the long, glass outline of Crombie's Garden centre came into view. A large horticulture complex set on the northern outskirt of Royston, Hertfordshire. One of those

Aladdin's caves that sold everything from small brown plastic pots to conservatories to full grown trees.

'Splendid place,' the Professor beamed. 'Can I pick up a bag of multi-purpose compost while I am here, Peter?'

'No.'

'Please, as we are here.'

The Chief Inspector stared hard at his pal.

'Only if you can find a clean bag. I am not having earth all over my clean boot.'

He turned rapidly.

'Excuse me,' he called to a young lad in green overalls pushing a wheelbarrow, 'Can you tell me where Paul Knowles is to be found?'

The young lad looked vacantly at Peter.

'He shares an office down at the end of the centre. You can try there.'

'Thank you,' the Chief Inspector replied.

He turned to the Professor.

'Once upon a time they would have gone and found him for you.'

'You and I started to shave, date girls and the Beatles burst onto the scene. Dangerous to remember old times, Peter,' the Professor said with a wry smile.

The two wandered through the enormous glazed garden centre to the rear offices.

'Paul Knowles?' the Chief Inspector asked.

'Next door,' the lad said munching his doorstop-sized sandwich.

'Paul Knowles?' the Chief Inspector repeated as he poked his head into the second doorway. There were two men on their lunch-break.

'Yes,' one of the young man cried looking round from the newspaper that he was reading.

'Chief Inspector Meadows and this is Professor Wellbelove,' he gestured. 'We are here about your mother's death.'

'Oh please sit down,' the young man replied, pulling over two grubby red plastic chairs.

'Do you want me to leave, Paul?' the other man asked rising from his seat.

'No, it is your lunchbreak. Finish your sandwich.'

'Okay, if that is alright?' he glanced at the Chief Inspector, who nodded.

Paul Knowles had keen icy-blue eyes and a pleasant smile. A young man in his early-thirties, wearing the obligatory green Crombie overalls.

'How can I help you?'

'First can we offer our condolences on your mother's death on Tuesday.'

'Thank you.'

'I didn't see you at the hospital on Tuesday?' the Chief Inspector recollected.

'No...I arrived there the next morning. I wasn't in on the Tuesday evening – Spanish evening classes. Then I stayed the night at a friend's house. I only got home at seven o'clock and that's when I saw the note and phoned the police station.'

'How well did you get on with your mother?' the Chief Inspector asked.

'My mother? She was alright.'

'I gather you were having an argument over the car you and your father restored – an Austin Healey 3000.'

'Just a mild squabble. I devoted a lot of man-hours to its restoration. I felt it should automatically have been mine on my father's death.'

'Of course, it is now,' Peter said pointedly.

'Yes, I suppose so.'

'I understand that you threatened to take your mother to court over *this mild squabble.*'

'Oh, idle threats said in the heat of the moment,' he said trying to dismiss the subject.

The Chief Inspector looked over at the Professor.

'Do you know if your mother had any enemies, Mr Knowles?' the Professor asked.

'I don't believe so. Everyone liked her.'

'Well, someone clearly didn't,' the Chief Inspector interjected.

'Did your late mother get on well with Angela Galbraith?' the Professor asked.

'They loved one another. Angela is a real sweetheart. My mother was pleased to move in and look after her.'

'Do you know anything about aconite?' the Professor asked.

'Monk's hood or wolf's bane,' Paul Knowles replied. 'I know a little.'

'Have you got any here?'

'No, a bit dodgy.'

'Yes we have Paul, down in the special compound,' his fellow worker said.

He turned to the Chief Inspector.

'It is highly poisonous so we keep it locked in a compound with other dangerous plants. Customers can only go in there with a member of staff.'

'Thank you,' the Chief Inspector replied.

A nice comprehensive answer which Paul Knowles didn't look too pleased about.

'Yes, I was forgetting. I thought we had stopped selling it,' he smiled awkwardly.

'You called into Angela's flat on Tuesday morning?' the Chief Inspector asked.

'Yes, I had a present for her. I had found a pair of earrings in a jeweller in Cambridge, just like the one that she had lost.'

'Green peridot,' the Professor interjected.

'Yes, that's the one. It was her favourite. I saw a nearly identical pair in a jeweller's window.'

'How did you know it was nearly identical. Have you an eye for jewellery?' the Professor asked.

'Oh not really. But Angela gave me a signed photo of herself from some fashion shoot and she was wearing them on that. So I knew exactly what they looked like.'

'And you were at Spanish evening classes on Tuesday evening?'

'That's right 7:30 – 10:00pm at Brinkley College.'

'Who is your tutor?'

'Señora Gabrielle Maria Diaz.'

'Your accent is good,' the Professor complimented. 'Señora Diaz has taught you well.'

'Thank you.'

'So you were at Brinkley College until ten o'clock and then where did you go, Mr Knowles?' the Chief Inspector asked.

'I walked to a pub in the city where I met my girlfriend. We had a drink and stayed there until eleven. Then we went back to her flat. I left there about seven o'clock and called into my flat, where I saw your note. That brings us back to where we started this conversation.'

'How did you manage to go to Angela's flat on Tuesday morning at ten thirty? Were you not at work that day?' the Professor asked.

'Early lunch hour,' he smiled. 'I had got into work at six thirty to do an unloading. So I had an early lunch-break about quarter past ten. Just enough time to get to Angela's and get back.'

'And you haven't been there since?' the Chief Inspector asked.

'No, I guess I will have to go there some time to collect Mum's clothes. I suppose there won't be many.'

'Okay, Mr Knowles, that will be all for the moment. We will get in touch if we need to clarify anything further.'

They all shook hands.

As they wandered back to the car, George grabbed a garden trolley.

'Oh not your bloody compost, George.'

'Just take five minutes.'

'I will come with you to make sure you get a clean one. Perhaps the girl at the checkout might have a damp cloth as well.'

With the clean sack of compost secured within his boot, the Chief Inspector pulled the slip of paper Angela had written out.

'Next suspect,' he grinned.

He dialled Dave Saunders's mobile phone.

'Can I phone you back, I am just under a bath at present,' the caller snapped.

'No you can't. This is Chief Inspector Meadows of the Cambridgeshire Constabulary.'

'Sorry, mate, I don't care who you are, you will have to wait your turn – I am very busy. I will phone you back in five minutes.'

'This is a murder enquiry and you are a suspect.'

There was a silence at the other end of the phone.

'Who did you say this was?'

'Chief Inspector Meadows of the Cambridgeshire Constabulary.'

'Is this some sort of wind-up? Is that you Sammy? I'll fucking have yer guts if it is.'

'No, this is a genuine Police enquiry. I need to come and talk to you, Mr Saunders, straight away. Where are you working?'

There was another silence.

'I'm at 15 Fossgate Gardens, Chesterton.'

'Stay there, I am coming straight over.'

The Chief Inspector spotted Dave Saunders's white transit parked outside No 15. It had to be - no other sensible tradesman would consider using the title - *Plumb-Crazy.*

The Chief Inspector and the Professor were greeted at the door by a stocky young man in his early thirties in a white boiler suit. He smoothed his hair back and oozed a huge Hollywood-type smile. Clearly he hadn't shaved that morning, though that might be designer-stubble. He had a very self-opinionated air about him, which immediately got up Peter's nose.

The Professor studied the young man and a shiver ran down his spine. He felt that the young man had cruel eyes.

'Mr David Saunders?' the Chief Inspector enquired as he held his police ID card at head height.

'Yes,' the gent replied apprehensively.

'This is my colleague, Professor Wellbelove from Cambridge University.'

'Pleased to meet you,' he said shaking their hands. 'You said over the phone about a murder?'

'That's right, Mrs Margaret Knowles.'

'Who's that. I don't know anyone of that name.'

'Angela Galbraith's aunt - the one staying at her flat.'

'So, someone's done the old cow...I mean lady in? She was miserable old ........lady.'

'Can we come in? I am sure you would prefer not to talk on the doorstep.'

'Yeah, the house is empty. I am putting in a new boiler for the people moving in next week.'

'Sorry, there's no furniture, so, I can't offer you gents a chair to sit on.'

'We can just stand in the hallway,' the Chief Inspector said dismissively.

'So who done the old girl in?' Dave Saunders asked when they had formed into a circle in the hallway.

'That's what we are trying to establish.'

'Can't be Angela, she was a sweet soul.'

'How long had you known her?'

'Angela? About a month. I put in a new bathroom suite – toilet and basin for her.'

'Still seeing her?'

'Oh yes, she was really good in the sack. Yeah, they say these posh girls like a bit of rough.'

The Professor grimaced. He turned his head slightly towards Peter – he knew from experience that Peter would react strongly to such a comment.

'Do they?' he replied. 'I guess a bit like someone looking forward to vomiting.'

The Professor turned his head away and smiled.

Dave Saunders wasn't quite sure what to make of the comment.

'Yes, I guess so,' he finally muttered.

'When did you last see her?' the Chief Inspector asked.

'Angela? I guess sometime last week. It's hard to find time for all these dolls.'

'At her flat?'

'Yeah, though the old gal didn't like me I got the icy cold shoulder treatment each time I called in. She even called me an uncouth lout to my face.'

'Surprising,' responded the Chief Inspector with a false smile.

'So I go where I am wanted. Plenty more clams in the sea – if you get my drift. But the old gal's gone now.' He sucked the air in between his teeth. 'Poor cow...er lady.'

'Did you bear Mrs Knowles any malice for getting in your way, when Angela got back from her skiing holiday?'

'Nah, Angela was a bit incarnated –'

'I think you mean incapacitated,' the Professor corrected.

'Oh yeah, thank, she was a bit incapacitated, so mattress dancing was not high on the agenda,' he laughed.

'I have to ask this, Mr Saunders, where were you on Tuesday night?'

'This Tuesday?'

He screwed his face up and rubbed his chin.

'Tuesday, down at the Royal Oak playing darts. We are in the league down there.'

'Do you play arrows, Chief Inspector?'

'No, not as a rule.'

'So you haven't been near the flat,' the Chief Inspector recapped. 'Do you have any customers or work in Marlborough Court?'

'Nah, bit snooty up there. Most have annual service contracts with British Gas and the like.'

'Okay, Mr Saunders, thank you for your time. I have your number if there are any further questions,' the Chief Inspector said as he shook hands.

The two sauntered down the path to the Chief Inspector's car.

'Not your sort of person, Peter?' the Professor grinned.

'Bumptious, cocksure prat. Thinks he is God's gift to womanhood.'

'Do you think he's not aware that Angela has blown him away or is he just not admitting it?' the Professor asked.

'Probably damage his male-ego to think any female could dare to contemplate dumping him,' the Chief Inspector snarled.

'He had cruel eyes,' the Professor declared. 'Do you think he might be our killer or Angela's associate?'

'I doubt if he could even spell aconite, let alone use it.'

Peter slowly calmed down.

'Let's see what Roger has found on the CCTV footage. Mr Plumb-Crazy said he hasn't been near the flat for a while. Let's see if any of the security cameras have picked up him or his van.'

The Chief Inspector set off in a southerly direction for the short drive back to Parkside Police Headquarters. Albeit with a quick detour to drop-off the sack of multi-purpose compost in Windermere Close.

When he got back to his office, he glanced through the glass partition into the adjoining office – Roger wasn't back.

'Well, George, it has been an interesting couple of hours,' the Chief Inspector said as he took off his jacket and hung it on the coat rack. He lowered himself into his office chair.

The Professor sat down in the chair in front of the desk.

'So Paul Knowles or Dave Saunders?' he enquired.

The Professor shrugged his shoulders.

'Either, for different reasons.'

The Chief Inspector leaned back in his chair and stared up at the ceiling.

'My money is on Paul Knowles. He has access to aconite and is family.'

'I really don't see Angela Galbraith coming under the spell of either. Neither are Rasputin-type of characters. Although Mr Plumb-Crazy comes close.'

'No, I go for Paul Knowles. All we haven't seen is the chemistry between him and Angela when they are together. That would seal it up for me.'

Peter lowered his eyes to look at his colleague.

'You may be right,' the Professor conceded. 'Okay starting with Paul Knowles, let's walk-through the case as we see it. At the flat, we are suggesting that Angela handed the missing bottle to Paul who disposed of it. What we need to do now is run this bond between them back to the instigation of the crime.

Despite the twaddle he told us, Paul Knowles wanted his Austin Healy. His mother wasn't playing ball, a court would probably rule in her favour, so the way to get his hands on it, was to inherit it. That meant Margaret Knowles had to die. Paul had monkshood growing at his garden centre – a fact he tried to hide.'

The Chief Inspector nodded.

'So he has the poison,' the Professor continued, 'and Angela the opportunity. We know that the two are very close - her uncle said that to Roger. Angela has sprung to his defence and called him a *sweetie* on at least three occasions that I have witnessed. She gave him a signed photograph of herself which he keeps in his flat.....Peter, they are very close - unhealthily close.'

'What you mean sexually?' Peter gulped.

'Whatever.'

The Professor raised an eyebrow.

'Cousins are rich courting material. The royal families of Europe have spent most of the last millennium marrying cousins. Let's face it, Prince Philip is the second or third cousin of the Queen.'

The Chief Inspector steepled his hands on his chest as he leaned back again.

'Okay, let's go with the premise that Angela Galbraith will do whatever Paul Knowles asks her to do...even murder. The two maybe gambling that as we would see that Angela has no clear motive and that there is no poison bottle in the flat, she wouldn't be charged.'

'That's one hell of a risky strategy,' the Professor groaned.

'But one, Paul may have convinced her to take,' the Chief Inspector said resolutely.

The Chief Inspector leant forward and stared at his colleague.

'What do we need George?'

'Simply, evidence that Paul Knowles was at Marlborough Court on Tuesday evening.'

'Okay, that's Paul Knowles, what about Mr Plumb-Crazy?'

'I guess the leverage is sexual-violence – the hold aggressive men have over women. Dave Saunders may hold some sort of perverse power over Angela. Perhaps she does like a bit of rough love-making.'

'Have you renewed your subscription to something that you haven't told me about, George?'

'Peter, masochists do walk this earth.'

'So, Dave Saunders uses some sort of unsavoury leverage to get Angela to do what he wants?'

'In a nutshell. You think of the Stockholm Syndrome, where a victim becomes infatuated with their abductor. We are a complicated bunch.'

'Okay, Mr Plumb-Crazy remains in the frame,' the Chief Inspector agreed.

He looked across to the adjoining office.

'Right,' Peter cried slapping the palms of his hands down on his desk. 'Where's Roger?'

At that moment a smartly dressed lady knocked and came in with the Chief Inspector's post.

'Do you know where Sergeant Carter is, Valerie?'

'He phoned-in quarter of an hour ago and said he was on his way back here.'

'Good, I would rather like to see him sooner, rather than later.'

She smiled and collecting up the paperwork in Peter's "Out" tray, she departed.

'Thanks, George, it looks like your little grey cells are getting us to a point where we can see the case in sharp focus.'

The Professor smiled.

'And got Dorothy and I a sack of compost for the garden.'

'Shhhhhh. No shouting about that at the University. It is strictly against the rules to use police vehicles to run errands.'

There was a knock on the door and they turned to see Roger's smiling face.

'Oh, speak of the Devil,' the Chief Inspector cried. 'It is Steven Spileberg.'

'I wish it were, sir.'

'Why do you say that?'

'The security cameras don't work.'

'What none of them?'

The Sergeant shook his head.

'It took me ages to get the name of the property management company. I decided to start talking to the residents on the other wing hoping one of them might have a telephone contact number. Finally, one of them had a number. Can I sit down sir, it's been a long day.'

'Certainly,' Peter gestured to the spare chair.

'I spoke to someone at their office, who transferred me to one of their directors,' Roger glanced at his notebook, 'A Mr Anthony Silverman. He explained that the company that installed the cameras went bust in the middle of the job. Another company came in and ripped out all their wiring and replaced it with their superior type. So, the system was finally installed, but there was now an argument as to who was meant to commission it. The second company said they were only paid to install it; the first company had been paid to commission it – but they had gone bust.'

'That is nearly ten years ago,' the Chief Inspector exclaimed.

He looked across at the Professor who raised an eyebrow.

'So we have no CCTV footage at Marlborough Court at all?'

'Afraid not.'

'I wonder if the residents know they haven't got a security camera system?' the Chief Inspector groaned.' They nearly rioted over an improper access-code, they will be setting fire to cars and smashing shop windows at this news.'

The Chief Inspector leaned back in his chair and stared up at the ceiling.

'Well, perhaps a slight over-exaggeration, but it is a poor deal....and for the inflated price they paid for their up-market flats.'

He turned to his Sergeant.

'You said you spoke to some of the residents this afternoon, did they see anything going on in Flat 311 on Tuesday night?'

'Nothing so far.'

'We're not getting very far with this case. We have a lot of theories but no proof,' the Chief Inspector groaned.

'Shame about the cameras,' the Professor sighed. 'I guess we are back to good old police detective work – two alibis to check out?'

The Professor rose and wandered over to the window. He looked across the beautiful expanse of grass called Parker's Piece, set in the heart of the great city.

'We're assuming one of them came to the flat and took the bottle,' the Professor gripped the window sill and closed his eyes. He wandered down the long dark passages of his mind. 'I guess it could actually be someone else.'

'What? A neighbour?' the Chief Inspector said in surprise as he turned to look at his colleague.

'Anyone until the ambulance men arrived……

The Professor's voice trailed away.

'Of course, it could one of the ambulance men that took the bottle?' the Professor cried as he straightened up and turned. He had that look in his eyes.

'A third member of the gang? the Chief Inspector cried. 'You will have a cast greater than Cecile B. DeMille's "Ten Commandments" at this rate, George.'

'It is the cornerstone of this case. The person who came to the flat and spirited away the poison bottle is a principal player in this conspiracy.'

George was still thinking about that point when he helped Dorothy clear away the plates, cups and saucers and cutlery from the dinner table.

While she loaded the dishwasher, George opened the cupboard and began taking out the small containers and bottles.

'You are meant to be helping me clear up, not making more mess, George,' she smiled. 'What are you looking for?'

'A poison bottle.'

'What? In *our* cupboard?'

'No, at a murder scene.'

Dorothy was quite relieved to hear it.

'How do you hide one or get rid of it?' he puzzled.

'I am sure that you have already considered all the suggestion that I could possibly come up with, dear,' she said.

'Did you think of posting it to yourself?' she muttered as she closed the dishwasher door.

'Funnily enough, no.'

She smiled.

'Or better still, post it to a company that makes glass bottles in South America. They would be mystified for weeks about its arrival. And if there was no return address, I guess they would eventually throw it away. Job done.'

'Well, while you are on your knees, George, can you get the washing powder out of the cupboard next to you. I want to put some washing on.'

Dorothy disappeared upstairs and returned with an armful of soiled washing.

She found George staring at a washing detergent capsule on the worktop, which he repeatedly kept prodding.

'It's a washing capsule, George. It saves me going to the stream and bashing the clothes with large smooth rocks. I just throw one of those at it instead,' she chuckled.

'I wonder what it is made of?'

'Washing detergent.'

'No, the plastic gel pouch.'

'I don't know. It just dissolves in the washing machine and the clothes come out sparkling white. Well, at least those that went in white.'

'It is some sort of water-soluble gel,' he said, prodding it again.

'If it is that fascinating, you can take one and play with in in your study. No, on second thoughts after that disaster with that mug of coffee, it stays in here.'

The Professor ignored the comment.

'I wonder if you could drain it and put aconite in it? A fine syringe, perhaps?'

Dorothy loaded the washing machine with all the washing that she had carried down. She put fabric freshener in the slide-out tray and turned and stared at her husband.

'Can I have the one you are playing with or are you two going to get married?'

The Professor chuckled.

'No, I have seen enough.'

He kissed her on the cheek.

'Washing capsules and South America – two new leads for Peter,' he jabbered as he waltzed off to his study.

South America could wait, but washing detergent capsules were still on the Professor's mind, when he called in to see *Grumpy Jack*, Forensic Pathologist the next morning.

'Why doesn't the washing detergent inside dissolve the washing capsules pouch?'

'Laundry? The wife's department,' Jack growled and turned away with a dismissive wave of his arm.

'No, seriously, Jack, what dissolves them?'

He turned and stared at the Professor.

'Giving up teaching and going into the laundry business, are we?'

'It's regarding Margaret Knowles's murder.'

'Oh, that,' he frowned, 'Nasty case of aconite poisoning.'

'Could you empty a washing detergent capsule and fill it with aconite?'

'What? Are you intending to murder your washing machine?' he babbled.

'We have a missing poison bottle and I was wondering if you could put the poison in one of those water soluble capsules?'

'Oh, I see the reason for the daft question. They are made of a material called Polyvinyl Alcohol.'

'Could you fill one with aconite?' the Professor asked.

Grumpy Jack pouted.

'Need to experiment with that...and v-e-r-y carefully.'

'So it is possible?'

'Possible, but the material is designed to dissolve in warm water and with agitation, just as you find inside a washing machine. A cold glass of vodka is a completely different environment.'

The Professor stepped in a wide circle, head downcast as he pondered the scenario.

'All finished?' Jack called out as he washed his hands, ready for the next task.

'Did you do the autopsy on Margaret Knowles?'

'No, a colleague did it up at Addenbrooke's. I just got a copy of the report for our files.'

'Anything done here?'

'Mainly the team next door who examined everything the SOCO boys brought over from Old Mother Hubbard's Kitchen Cupboard. I did examine Margaret's glass personally.'

'What did you find?'

'A high concentration of aconite in a solution of vodka and citric acid – which I believe was the bitter lemon.'

'You said high concentration?'

'Yes, there were splashes on the inside of the glass. It was highly toxic, perhaps concentrated by someone to a very high level. In that form, it would have enough potency to kill an elephant.'

'A hard thing to do?'

'What? Killing an elephant or concentrating aconite?'

'Concentrating aconite,' George tutted.

'No, not if you know what you are doing.'

'A chemist, a pharmaceutical graduate or someone in the medical field?'

'Someone like that. Certainly not a ten-year-old school boy with a chemistry set.'

'Any other features of note about the glass, Jack?'

The pathologist shook his head.

'A smear of lipstick around one part of the rim, one set of fingerprints – Margaret Knowles and a few paper fibres.'

'Paper fibres?'

'Yes, I understand Margaret Knowles poured out the drinks and I can only assume that she wiped the glasses with a piece of damp kitchen paper before she poured out the drinks.'

'Modern dishwashers do leave glasses smeary – even with rinse aid.'

'Gosh, George, you would be a natural in a laundry,' Jack joked.

'Nothing unexpected then?'

'Oh, I did find a tiny triangle of plastic in her glass – sides about half a centimetre.'

'A quarter of an inch? That is minute.'

'I thought it was cling-film at first, but I detected a sticky residue on one surface. So I believe it is a corner of adhesive tape or the like.'

'Probably the security plastic round the neck of the vodka or bitter lemon bottles. '

The Professor thought for a second.

'Hold on, they both had ice in their drinks. Ice cubes can be made in those plastic ice cube bags that you fill with water and then freeze. A bit of one of those might have stuck to an ice cube when they were popped out.'

'Oh, not just laundry, your expertise extends to home freezing as well. Delia Smith watch out George Wellbelove will be after your job,' he chuckled.

'Anything else, Jack?'

The Pathologist shook his head.

'Found your murderer yet? he asked.

'Yes and no. We have a theory.'

'Excellent. Sir Isaac Newton started like that. He studied at Trinity College down the road, you know?.'

As the Professor was about to leave, he paused and turned.

'Jack, is there any way, aconite could be administered but its effect delayed by, say, twelve hours?'

'Like in those slow-release cold and flu capsules that the bile in the stomach eats away at?'

'Yes,' the Professor said excitedly.

'Have you got access to the labs of Roche, Pfizer or Glaxo Smith Kline?'

'No.'

'Then the answer, George is equally no.'

The Professor strolled out of the Pathology lab in a slightly dispirited fashion.

'Theories and no facts.,' he muttered.

Only Angela Galbraith could have administered the poison but, like Peter had said in the beginning, she was an amiable and sweet girl. Even under Paul Knowles's or Dave Saunders's influence he couldn't see her as a cold-blooded killer.

He looked at his wristwatch.

'Can't hang around, tutorial at ten thirty,' he thought as he strode down the pavement. 'I will give Peter a call this afternoon.'

George was back in his office at the university after a stimulating lecture when the phone rang.

'Oh, Peter, I was just about to phone you.'

'Telepathy, Dr Watson,' Peter joked.

'What's new with Margaret Knowles's murder?' the Professor asked.

'Well Dave Saunders's alibi doesn't hold up. The landlord of the Royal Oak said the Dave missed the darts match on Tuesday.'

'Really?'

'He knows for certain, as his son had to take his place.'

'Okay, but does that put him in the frame?'

'Paul Saunders also has a record – GBH and armed robbery.'

'Bloody hell,' George exclaimed. 'I said that he had cruel eyes.'

'There's more,' Peter added.

'Not that he has a violent hatred of old ladies?'

'No, this is our other friend Paul Knowles. The College can't find the attendance register for his evening class. It's not in the rack.'

'With Señora Gabrielle Maria Diaz?'

'She's on a week's leave and flew back to Spain - her father is unwell.'

'So either of them could be a mysterious gentleman-caller at the flat?'

'Could be.'

'Peter, is there a post box outside of Marlborough Court?'

'I haven't a clue. Why do you ask?'

'Just wondering if Angela could have posted anything.'

'What like a poison bottle?'

'Precisely.... especially to South America.'

'Why South America?'

'Oh, it just gets it far, far away.'

'So what's next?' the Professor asked.

'Well, Roger has gone to collect Dave Saunders and I have asked Paul Knowles to call in on his way home.'

'Need me at all?'

'No, this is pure police work, George. You know, darkened room, spotlight in the suspect's face and a short length of rubber hose held discretely behind my back,' he joked.

Twenty minutes later the Chief Inspector's phone rang.

'Roger, sir. I have Dave Saunders in Interview room 2.'

'I will be down.'

The Chief Inspector strode into the interview room to find Dave Saunders slouched in the chair on the far side of the table.

'Here we are again,' Dave said wittily.

'What since yesterday?' the Chief Inspector said putting his papers on the table and not giving the visitor the courtesy of looking at him.

'No, I was meaning that I am back in my favourite Mastermind chair. "And you have two minutes on your specialist subject, Mr Saunders – armed robberies of the twentieth century." '

The Chief Inspector sat down and fixed the young man with a harsh stare.

'There is no need to pretend, Chief Inspector,' Dave Saunders groaned, 'you know my history and I have done stir.'

The Chief Inspector nodded. His face still expressionless.

'But that is all behind me, I have paid my debt to Society,' he said smugly.

The Chief Inspector turned the page of the report he was reading.

'Interviewed in connection with stolen goods last year,' he said quietly.

'Oh, they only wanted to know if I had heard anything. I have my ear to the ground.'

The Chief Inspector closed the file.

'Anyway, we are not here to discuss your criminal record. I need to inform you that your alibi for Tuesday night doesn't hold up. You told me yesterday that you were at the Royal Oak in a darts tournament.'

'That's right.'

'The landlord of the Royal Oak says that you didn't turn up.'

'He's got a bad memory. We won 6-2.'

'And his son had to take your place.'

Dave Saunders looked wrong-footed.

'Oh, I guess I am getting my Tuesdays muddled up. That must have been the previous Tuesday. Nah, this Tuesday I was with a friend.'

'Male or female?'

'Female.'

'And may I ask where?'

'At her house.'

'And her name?'

'I would rather not say.'

'Why?'

' 'Cos she's married.'

The Chief Inspector put down his pen and stared hard at the young Lothario.

    'Mr Saunders, it might have escaped your attention, but we are trying to establish an alibi for you to actually eliminate any possibility that you were in the vicinity of a murder at Marlborough Court. This lady will provide that alibi.'

    'I still would prefer to leave her out of it.'

The Chief Inspector folded his arms.

    'Irrespective of your views, police officers can be tactful and discrete in their questioning.'

    'If you say so.'

The Chief Inspector took a long deep breath. He spread his hands out on the table.

    'It is a trade-off - her confirmation of your alibi or you are in the frame for murder, Mr Saunders.'

Dave Saunders stared hard at his adversary.

    'Her old man is a copper.'

Peter had not expected that comment. He drew on all his strength to not let any emotion cross his face or fill his eyes.

He took another deep breath.

    'I will need her name in order for her to provide your alibi,' the Chief Inspector said calmly.

Dave Saunders paused and grimaced.

    'Her name is Babs....Barbara Monroe.'

    'Barbara Monroe,' the Chief Inspector repeated as unemotionally as he could.

The Chief Inspector had known Sergeant Dickie Monroe for over ten years. He had also met Barbara socially. A very attractive woman with long curly brunette hair and a large bust. She struck him as lively and outgoing, but not a woman to cross-the-line – especially with the likes of Dave Saunders.

'Will you say anything to her husband?' Dave asked.

'Nothing to do with me. It is a matter between the two of them. But I would recommend that you end your liaison.'

'I am not the first...nor the last - '

'- Mr Saunders, that is their affair and nothing to do with anyone else,' the Chief Inspector interrupted.

He closed the folder in front of him. He had a nasty taste in his mouth.

'If it checks out, you have an alibi.'

He rose to his feet and, with no civility, turned and headed for the door.

'That is all for the moment, Mr Saunders,' he called over his shoulder. 'Roger, escort Mr Saunders off these premises.'

The Chief Inspector strode out of the room.

He returned upstairs. He pulled off his jacket as he strode down the corridor, unbuttoning his collar and pulling his tie to one side. He threw open the door to his office and without switching on the light, headed for his office chair. He flopped heavily into the seat. He sat in the darkness with his eyes closed.

When Peter was a young police officer and worked nights, his lovely wife was always a concern that he had at the back of his mind. But he and Rita had a good marriage – they survived.

A police officers job is difficult one, to say the least. Add in matrimonial pressures and it becomes harder than most can cope with.

Peter opened his eyes and logged into his computer. He called up the duty rota. He scanned down the list until he got to 'M'. His finger ran across the screen - Sergeant Richard Monroe was on the night shift this week. That was all he needed to know; all that he wanted to know.

He closed his eyes again.

The buzz of the telephone interrupted his thoughts. He wasn't sure if he had fallen asleep. He picked up the phone.

'Paul Knowles downstairs in Interview Room 1, sir,' Roger informed him.

'I will be straight down.'

He pulled open his drawer and unwrapped an extra strong mint. Something to take the nasty flavour of Dave Saunders out of his mouth.

He walked down the corridor again, pulling on his jacket and straightening his tie.

'Mr Knowles, thank you for coming in,' he greeted his visitor as if he didn't have a care in the world. Peter was a professional.

'I will come straight to the point as undoubtedly you want to get home. It would appear that your Señora Diaz has taken the class register with her to Spain.'

'Spain?'

'Her father is apparently unwell. So I don't know if classes will be cancelled next week or you will have a different teacher,' Peter added.

'Right, I will phone the college. Thanks for letting me know.'

'It's about your alibi for last Tuesday. As we can't verify that you were at Brinkley College, can you tell us what pub you and your lady went to? And her name would be useful.'

The Chief Inspector took out a pen from his inside jacket pocket.

'It was The Mill in Mill Lane. My girlfriend is Zoe Carmichael, she's in the Halls of Residence at Clare College.'

'First year undergraduate?'

'Yes.'

After Dave Saunders's revelation, the Chief Inspector was not going to broach the subject of a thirty-year old man having a nineteen-year-old girlfriend. He would tack into safer waters.

'There's three years difference in ages between you and Angela Galbraith?'

'Yes, both born in August – both Leos,' he smiled.

'See eye to eye on most things?'

'Leos from the same family, yes, you would expect that to be so.'

'Can you persuade her to do most things, or is she very strong-willed?'

'She's easy-going, but can be stubborn.'

'Manipulable?'

'Not really. I don't get your drift.'

'Could you persuade her to murder someone?'

'Good God, no, Chief Inspector,' he exclaimed rising from his seat.

'Sit down, Mr Knowles,' the Chief Inspector said quietly as he flicked through the folder in front of him.

'Mr Knowles I still have a huge problem to overcome. Angela Galbraith was the only person in the flat with your late mother when she was poisoned. You told me yesterday that she was a real sweetheart. Are you two close?'

'As close as any two cousins can be.'

'Has it ever gone beyond that?'

'Such as what?'

'Do you hug and kiss one another at Christmas?'

'Sometimes.'

'Big hugs and long kisses?'

'Chief Inspector what are you suggesting?'

'I am asking if you and Angela ever slept together?'

'That's obscene and monstrous.'

'Why? She is very attractive.'

'Haven't you two been alone and felt an uncontrollable urge?'

'No never.'

'Not fantasised about the exquisite taste of forbidden fruit?'

'What? With my own sister,' he shrieked.

The Chief Inspector's jaw dropped. That one he didn't see coming.

The two stared at one another in silence. The Chief Inspector was determined to let Paul Knowles speak first. To be honest he wasn't entirely sure what he would say, anyway.

>'Rex Galbraith is my father,' Paul finally muttered.

>'Who told you that?' the Chief Inspector asked coolly.

>'My father, just before he died.'

Peter took a deep breath, he thought Dave Saunders's revelation was enough for one day – now he had a second exposé.

>'My father had his suspicions at the time of my birth, as he was abroad a lot, but as I grew older, he could see Rex's eyes in mine. That said, he loved me and cared for me as if I was his.'

>'Who knew that you knew?'

>'Only my father and Angela.'

>'How did she know?'

>'I told her.'

>'Was she upset?'

>'Quite the reverse, she was happy to have a brother.'

>'You never spoke to your mother about it?'

>'No.'

The Chief Inspector closed the folder on the table. There might be numerous more questions to ask, but his head was spinning – he need time to reflect or a large glass of whiskey....or both.

>'The purpose of coming in tonight is to re-establish your alibi for Tuesday evening. I think we have wandered off that just

a shade. But I make no apologies for that in that we now know clearly your relationship to Angela Galbraith.'

Paul Knowles nodded.

'Roger, here,' the Chief Inspector pointed over his shoulder, 'will make contact with the landlord of The Mill and Miss Carmichael. Hopefully that will offset Señora Diaz poor administration skills.'

The Chief Inspector rose to his feet. Paul Knowles followed suit.

'Mr Knowles thank you for coming in and also being honest with us. I know it hasn't been easy for you. Thank you.'

'Roger, please show Mr Knowles out and then come and see me in my office.'

The Chief Inspector climbed the stairs again, perhaps a little more wearily than before.

He slumped in his chair.

'Thank goodness there aren't any more interviews – I not sure I could cope with more infidelity,' he muttered.

Sergeant Carter wandered into the office.

'Okay, Roger, one question. Has either of those interviews thrown up a killer for Margaret Knowles?'

'Not sure, it has sir.'

'No, I'm not sure either,' he groaned.


The following morning, the Chief Inspector swept into the Professor's driveway, cornering against the tall privet hedge.

'You really ought to come onto this driveway more slowly,' the Professor reprimanded his friend.

'Sorry, I didn't know you would be out jogging.'

'I have just been up to the pillar box,' the Professor snapped.

'A lot to tell you, George, in the Margaret Knowles case.'

Without making any attempt to even reach George's study, the Chief Inspector stood, arms folded in the driveway and detailed the revelations of the previous evening.

The Professor listened avidly to Peter's summary.

'You did have a productive evening last night.'

'I got through half a packet of extra strong mints before I got home,' he groaned.

'So you have stripped away the rickety defences of our two would-be accomplices?' the Professor grinned.

'Three.'

'Who's the third?'

'Rex Galbraith – the man with a secret.'

'Surely, you don't think that secret wouldn't compromise his position at Addenbrooke's?'

'What if Eleanor didn't know and Margaret wanted to broadcast the news? He might have a motive to silence Margaret. Perhaps the revelation might damage his reputation? He is prominent individual, perhaps he wants to become an MP or go on a University board or the join the Church of England Synod or something. Okay you may have to be ordained for the last one. But you get my drift.'

'A bit over-the-top surely, Peter?'

'People have killed for a lot less, George.'

The Professor pondered the suggestion.

'Grumpy Jack did say that the aconite had been concentrated and Rex has the facilities at Addenbrooke's to do just that.'

'What about a three-way conspiracy? Paul gets the aconite from the garden centre, Rex concentrates it and Angela administers it?'

'Phew, the deadly-duo becomes the toxic-trio.' the Professor exclaimed.

'It's no joking matter, George,' the Chief Inspector snapped.

'No, I know. Let me think about that one for a couple of seconds.'

He folded his arms and looked away.

'Rex wants to silence Margaret, Paul wants to get his hands on his car and Angela is beaten into submission, figuratively speaking, by both her father and brother. A neat solution,' the Chief Inspector summarised.

'Sounds like a 1930 film noire movie,' the Professor commented.

'But it is not beyond the bounds of possibility?' the Chief Inspector pressed.

'It's feasible. But, as I said, it sounds more like Hollywood than Cambridge, England.'

The Professor absentmindedly let the toe of his brogue sweep a circle in the gravel.

' "The Man in the Corridor" is the lynch-pin in this murder,' he mused. 'Hold on, I have just had another thought.'

The familiar pained expression ran across his face as the grey cells went into overdrive.

'No need for an additional caller...... Angela's father, Rex, fits in rather nicely..........'

The Chief Inspector had to ask as the Professor wandered off down another dark tunnel in his brain.

'Why nicely, George?'

'Oh that is so neat,' George cried as a scheme unravelled in his mind.

'George, I can't mind-read, what is this nice, neat theory.'

He turned to Peter with a huge smile on his face.

'If Rex were "The Man in the Corridor", no one would have to make a special journey to the flat. When Rex and Eleanor arrived to take Angela to the hospital, she simply slipped the poison bottle into his hand when Eleanor wasn't looking. Bingo!'

'Then Rex has numerous ways to dispose of the bottle at the hospital the next morning,' the Chief Inspector added.

'Very neat, don't you think?' the Professor beamed.

'So Rex could be our "Man in the Corridor"?' the Chief Inspector enthused. 'Right, I need to talk to him.'

He glanced at the Professor but he was 'gone' again.

'I said I need to talk to him,' the Chief Inspector repeated.

'Of course it might be the "The Lady in the Corridor"?' George muttered.

'What Angela's mother?' said the Chief Inspector in disbelief.

'Yes,' said George resoundingly. 'What if Angela wasn't delighted that Paul was her brother? What if she found the idea abhorrent – her father and her Auntie Margaret - urghhh? What if she told her mother of Rex's affair and illegitimate son? Perhaps the two might have become incensed with the revelation?'

'*Heaven has no rage like love to hatred turned, Nor hell a fury like a woman scorned,*' the Chief Inspector quoted.

'So, rather than Rex, Angela and her mother hatched the plot to exact revenge. After the event Angela slipped the poison bottle to Eleanor. She spirited it away in her coat pocket or even her handbag.'

The Chief Inspector exhaled loudly.

'Let me start with Rex,' he said. 'I am sure by the time I have finished with him, you will have come up with another ten possibilities.'

The Professor smiled.

'Do you want me to come with you?'

The Chief Inspector shook his head.

'Thanks, but I don't want him to feel outnumbered and go on the defensive right from the start. I will see him in his office. I will get Valerie to make an appointment to see him at 10:30.'

'It's Saturday, Peter, will Valerie be there?'

'Oh yes, so it is. Perhaps I will get Rita to do that. She can do a posh secretary voice. I can meet him at his home - his study should be reasonably private.'

'Are you hoping to break him?'

'No, just to spook him.'

'Because I was going to say, of the three of them, he is least likely to spill the beans.'

'No, this is a multi-stage operation. Today is just spooking and softening up. If it is as we said, he might talk to the others and they may get jittery.'

Peter looked at his watch.

'Nearly nine o'clock,hmmmm. Did I hear the chink of a distant teapot?'

'No, you didn't. But I guess it could be arranged. Come inside.'

'I can give Rita a quick call then. I am very amiable and persuasive after I have had a digestive biscuit.'

'I will have a word to her and get her to buy a bulk stock of them,' George grinned.

'But yours always taste nicer.'

'The other man's grass always tastes sweeter,'

'Oh don't remind me of that topic, Dickie Monroe has been on my mind all night.'

The two wandered inside.

'Morning, Dorothy,' the Chief Inspector called out.

'Good Lord, the Bad-Penny turns up again,' she cried as she came down the stairs with the two empty cups and saucers in her hand from their morning tea. 'Do you want me to make up the spare bedroom for you? You must spend more time here than at your own home. Can you still remember where it is?'

'Just about,' he grinned. 'As you have the cups already in your hand - yes, a cup of tea would be wonderful.'

'This isn't Lyons Corner House, you know.'

'But you do make such exquisite cups of tea,'

'Were your grandparents Irish. Peter?'

'No, why?'

'Because it sounds like you have kissed the Blarney Stone more than a few times.'

'Oh be Jesus, be gone with you woman,' he said in a terrible Irish accent. He playfully patted her on the rump as she escaped into the kitchen.

'You'd better come into the study before you cause any more trouble,' the Professor chuckled.

'Give me two seconds,' he said pulling his mobile phone out of his pocket.

Hello, Rita, it's me,' he began. 'Can you play secretary for me?'

She said something and he went pink.

'Honey, I am with George at this moment, save that talk for later. No, what I was meaning was, put on your posh voice and make me an appointment with Rex Galbraith for 10:30 at his house. Okay? I will text you his number in a second. It's on this phone, but as I have that to my ear at present, it is a difficult manoeuvre...I would probably cut you off in the process,' he laughed. 'Okay, 10:30 at his house. Don't take no for an answer.'

He scrolled through the phone's address book, hit a couple of keys and returned the phone to his jacket pocket.

'So while you are tackling Rex Galbraith this morning, Peter, what's Roger doing?'

'He's down at Marlborough Court knocking on a few more doors.'

'Want me to do anything?'

'Not really.'

'Excellent, I will reassemble my Mappin & Webb carriage clock. Ah, the tea,' he cried as Dorothy stepped in to the study.

'What, no digestive biscuits?' Peter cried.

'I only have one pair of hands. If I had a tray I could have managed it.'

'You lost it?' Peter asked.

'No, his lordship has his clock parts spread out on it while they dry.'

'How dare clock parts take priority over digestive biscuits,' Peter howled.

'Get him his biscuits, dear, or he'll be a pain in the butt for the next half an hour.'

Dorothy put down the two cups and saucers and scurried away.

'Is it worth talking to Margaret's brother about the big family secret?' the Professor asked. 'He was quite forthcoming with Roger in the beginning.'

'Maybe, let's see how I get on with Rex.'

The biscuits arrived and Peter dived in. He took two and placed them in his saucer.'

'Did you see that, dear? Two and he wasn't even asked.'

'Well, here's two to make up,' she said putting two biscuits on George's saucer. 'Shall I get the train-set down from the loft for you two boys to play with later?'

'Oh yes, woo-woo,' Peter cried.

Somehow George's study, and perhaps George himself, allowed Peter a moment to escape the harsh and ruthless world of crime and criminals. He needed that.

'Do you know Peter, I am still mystified about Angela Galbraith's character.'

'In what way?'

'She's complicated, but I still can't see her as a murderess.'

'They said that about Myra Hindley,' Peter murmured as he dunked his biscuit.

The Professor gazed out of the window at his garden.

'Are you going to do anything about that Australian bloke, what was his name? .... Ben Masters?'

'No, he's got nothing to do with the case.'

'What about the magician guy, who sends Angela flowers?' George asked.

'And drives a Bentley,' Peter cried in an Eleanor-type voice 'Greg Rocco, no, again, nothing to do with the case.'

'Angela went out with him for three months; he might be able to throw some light on her personality, if there really is another darker one lurking in the background?'

'You can always ask.'

Peter looked up from his dunking.

'You seem to be really bothered by this George? Is this a genuine George-hunch or is it just you dotting the 'i's and crossing the 't's.?'

'Just a sixth-sense.'

'Well, Roger is down at Marlborough Court today If it is really bugging you, pop down and Roger can flash his police ID card and get you an audience. You never know, El Rocco might even do some magic tricks for you. You would enjoy that.'

'I can tell him about my Uncle Charlie who made props for magicians.'

'We won't be able to drag you two apart,' he laughed as he took his third digestive biscuit.

'I am counting,' George muttered.

The Chief Inspector finished his tea and rammed the final half a biscuit in his mouth.

'Well as much I find it almost impossible to drag myself away from your scintillating personality and your wife's amazing tea, I have work to do. I need to pop into Parkside and collect some forms before going and doing battle with Rex Galbraith.'

After the customary farewells, Peter returned to the real world.

He had mapped out in his mind how he would tackle Rex Galbraith. A few official forms and a bit of bluff wouldn't go amiss.

Dead-on ten thirty, the Chief Inspector rang on the doorbell.

As anticipated, Rex Galbraith opened the door.

'Morning, Chief Inspector. As I explained to your secretary, Angela isn't feeling very well this morning.'

'I am sorry to hear that, but it isn't her I want to talk to – it's you, sir.'

Eleanor Galbraith wandered down the hallway.

'Morning, Mrs Galbraith.'

'Angela isn't feeling very well this morning, Chief Inspector.'

'So I gather, but it is your husband that I wish to talk to.'

'Oh, shall we go into the lounge?' she gestured.

'No, just Mr Galbraith.'

'Oh.'

She looked like someone had just torn up her invitation to the Queen's garden party.

'Right,' she said, turned and headed back down the hallway.

'Shall we go to my study, Chief Inspector?'

Rex lead the way to a room on the front wing of the house and swung open the large oak door to his study. As the Chief Inspector had expected, the room was dominated by three huge bookcases of reference books.

'Please take a seat, Chief Inspector.'

He gestured to the black leather seat in front of his large walnut desk. He walked around the desk and sat down in his high-backed leather chair.

'I had your nephew, Paul Knowles, come and see me yesterday.'

'How is he? I really ought to go and see him.'

'He is putting on a brave face,' the Chief Inspector stated. 'But I am wondering if the grief of losing both parents in such a short period is affecting him badly.'

'Grief is a powerful emotion,' Rex affirmed.

He settled into his chair.

'So what do you want to talk to me about then, Chief Inspector?'

'There is something that Mr Knowles said to me.'

'Which was?'

'That you were his father.'

The expression on Rex's face was not dissimilar to having received a full-weight jab from Muhammad Ali.

Before Rex could speak, the Chief Inspector steered the conversation away from a direct assault.

'As you just said, grief is a powerful emotion that we each work out in different ways.'

'Er..yes,' Rex spluttered.

'What's your reaction?'

'It is nonsense.'

'No, not the assertion, Paul's state of mind?'

'Oh that? Chief Inspector, when a person grieves they bombard the mind with a torrent of conflicting emotions – loss, regret, blame, loneliness – the list is almost endless. Delusion is one condition of grieving individuals. In extremes, they will deny to themselves that the person has actually died.'

'Terrible how the mind finds ways to cope,' the Chief Inspector added.

'There is one delusion born out of being cast out alone in this world, akin to *erotomanic delusion*, which is where the individual believes a prominent person or celebrity is in love with them. This powerful delusion creates a make-believe story where someone becomes a parent-substitute. Anything to banish loneliness. Paul appears to be doing that.'

The Chief Inspector was not at all sure that he followed what Rex had just said, but he gave a confident grin.

'I knew it was something like that,' the Chief Inspector smiled. 'I just didn't have your medical knowledge to explain it.'

'I will talk to Paul. But probably, once the funeral is out of the way, he will get his feet on the ground on his own accord.'

Rex Galbraith rose to his feet.

'I am glad, Chief Inspector, that you have brought this to my attention. I will deal with it.'

'Excellent,' the Chief Inspector replied as he rose to his feet.

He gathered up his papers.

'Oh there is one thing, Mr Galbraith,' the Chief Inspector said. 'As Mr Knowles has recorded the assertion in his statement, I am duty-bound to check it out.'

'Is that absolutely necessary? With all respect to Paul, it is the ramblings of a deluded man.''

'I am afraid so. I have a signed court-order here,' he pulled a sheet of paper out of the folder sufficient only to show the judicial letterhead.' I will need a blood sample from both of you.'

The Chief Inspector released a placating smile.

'But then if it is the delusion speaking, we have nothing to worry about.'

He pushed the unrelated court-order back into the folder.

'Chief Inspector,' Rex Galbraith said slumping back into his seat. 'I don't know where to begin.'

The Chief Inspector, with an almost child-like expression of innocence on his face, sat down again.

'I dated both sisters, Margaret and Eleanor when I was a young beau. It was quite open and upfront with both of them. They were both exciting young ladies. It was difficult to decide which one I would prefer to marry. But, after a few months, I began to favour Margaret over her sister. However, one day, Eleanor announced that she was pregnant. That in many ways made my decision for me. I did the honourable thing and married her without delay. Eleanor had a miscarriage, so she says, but by then, we were wed.

Margaret found a smashing guy called Timothy Knowles and they got married. Tim, was a sales director for Hawker Siddeley and toured the world selling Trident airliners and other aircraft. Well, of course Margaret was left at home and on her own for a lot of time. I don't need to draw you a picture, Chief Inspector. Well, young people will be young people,' he smiled, but it was an apologetic smile.

'Paul was born to Margaret and Tim in 1985. Tim was over the moon. They looked a loving, happy family. It was only when Paul became a toddler that if one looked closely, his fair hair and pale blue eyes looked a shade out of keeping with Margaret and Tim's light brown eyes. But Tim was a fine father and doting parent.'

'Did he ever say anything to you or Margaret?'

Rex shook his head.

'I believed all these years that he never had the slightest doubt that Paul was his son.'

Rex let out a loud and emotional breath, as if by his confession a huge weight had been lifted off his shoulders.

'I assume Tim told Paul?' Rex asked.

'Just before he died.'

'God, he knew for all those years,' Rex gasped.

The two sat in silence for a few seconds staring down at the top of the desk. Rex quietly shook his head as he reviewed some of the mistakes of his life.

'Well, our family secret is out.'

The Chief Inspector nodded.

'Forgive me, I am not clear how this impacts on the case you are investigating?'

'It is just another dimension to Margaret Knowles.'

'But that is all?'

'Can I ask if your wife knows about Paul?' the Chief Inspector asked.

'No.'

'I would suggest that is one aspect we need to bear in mind.'

'Eleanor didn't kill her sister. We were both here all Tuesday evening.'

The Chief Inspector nodded without comment.

'One last point, I need to inform you that Paul said that he told Angela.'

'Oh, my God,' Rex cried.

'I must add that he said that she was delighted that he was her brother and not just a cousin.'

Rex didn't comment - he might have still been traumatised from the Chief Inspector's earlier revelation.

'Angela wouldn't have harmed Margaret. She loved her like I did.'

The Chief Inspector nodded again.

'When do you want me to do the blood-test, Chief Inspector?'

'I imagine that will be unnecessary now. I will be in touch if it is still required.'

He rose to his feet. He looked across at Rex Galbraith who looked decidedly grey; as if all the blood in his body had drained down into his socks.

Peter walked back to his car. He still got a kick out of arresting villains, but ruining normal decent people's lives with bad news was becoming a burden he found it harder to shoulder with each successive year.

The Professor was en-route to Marlborough Court. Curiosity had got the better of him. He wanted to talk to Greg Rocco about Angela. He had arranged to meet Roger on the third floor at eleven thirty.

'Morning, George,' Roger called from the other end of the corridor as the Professor stepped out of the lift.

'How have you been getting on this morning?' the Professor asked.

The Sergeant shook his head.

'No one saw anything untoward in Angela's flat on Tuesday. One lady said she saw Margaret Knowles come on to the balcony once, look around and then go back in. But other than that- zilch.'

'Well it was always a long-shot.'

'But a lot of police work is just that,' Roger said philosophically. 'You want to talk to Greg Willis, alias Greg Rocco?'

'Well, he might just be able to give us a tiny insight into Angela's character – they dated one another for three months last year.'

'He's in flat 347,' said Roger pointing down the corridor.

'Where's that in relation to Angela's flat?'

'Virtually opposite.'

The Professor nodded.

They walked to the flat and Roger banged loudly on the door.

There was silence for a few seconds, followed by a click as the bolt was slid back and the door opened about two inches. A man's face appeared in the gap.

'Yes.'

'Sergeant Carter, Cambridgeshire Constabulary,' Roger said as he held his ID wallet up to the gap.

'Yes,' the face repeated.

'And this is Professor Wellbelove from Cambridge University.'

'Yes,' the face repeated yet again.

'Can we come in?'

'Why?'

'We want to talk to you about Angela Galbraith.'

'It's not convenient, I have birds on the loose in here.'

Roger sensibly made no joke about scantily clad ladies running around the flat.

'It will only take about five minutes,' he said firmly. 'It is important.'

The face hesitated.

'Oh, alright. Give me a couple minutes to get my birds locked away.'

And the door closed.

'Cagy lot, these showbiz sorts,' Roger grinned.

'A trained bird can be worth a fortune to these professionals. They make or break an act,' the Professor said.

As they talked, the door opened again and a medium height, suntanned gentleman dressed in a black satin dressing gown and yellow slippers appeared in the doorway. A strong perfumed aroma flowed from his flat.

'How can I help you?' he asked.

'I would prefer not to talk in the corridor. Can we come in?' Roger said in a rather insistent tone.

The man shrugged his shoulders and without comment opened the door. With a huge theatrical sweep, he gestured them into his modest flat.

The Professor glanced out the corner of his eye at the gentleman as he walked past.

He was in his early forties with black hair that just didn't quite sit normally on his head – yet it didn't look a wig. But it was more the shiny skin on his face, which transfixed the Professor. He resembled an ochre-fleshed mannequin or perhaps a tailor's dummy with orange skin. Either way, it didn't look normal. The Professor accepted that on a stage and twenty feet away and under the right lighting, Rocco might look quite natural and presentable.

The Professor walked further into the flat; his eyes flicking from corner to corner. The flat was the mirror-image of Angela's flat. He also noted all the doors were shut. Not secretive, but perhaps with birds on the loose, that was only to be expected.

'Mr Willis, or would you prefer Rocco?' Roger asked politely.

'Rocco is my stage name and the one most people know me by,' he replied in an affected manner.

'Mr Rocco, we would like to talk to you about Angela Galbraith.'

A curious look ran across his face.

'You dated her for a few months last year,' the Professor interjected.

'A quaint term, dating,' Rocco said. 'We went to parties and dinner together.'

'Angela said it was a little more than that.'

'Oh did she, sweet child,' he smiled.

'I was meaning that you slept together,' the Professor said bluntly.

'That's what healthy men and women do, isn't it?'

'What I was driving at, was that you had a serious relationship and got to know one another quite well?'

'Fairly well.'

'How would you describe her temperament?' the Professor asked.

'Intelligent, sweet-natured, lovely smile and exquisite blue eyes.'

'You offered her a job as your assistant, didn't you?' Roger interrupted.

'Oh yes, she is just the right figure for the job - attractive, excellent legs, lovely arm gestures, slender and very gymnastic.'

'But she didn't take the job?' the Professor added,

'No, she signed up with that asshole Tony Warlock,' he hollered. 'He's all camera-tricks, not a proper magician, at all.'

'Not like Ali Bongo,' the Professor chortled.

'Oh not in his league,' Rocco smiled.

'Who's Ali Bongo?' Roger asked.

'Philistine,' Rocco shrieked. 'One of the great British magician, young man.'

'President of the Magic Circle,' George added. 'Real name William Oliver Wallace, died in 2009.'

'Oh, an aficionado who knows his magic,' Rocco positively glowed with admiration.

The Professor smiled confidently.

'My uncle, Uncle Charlie, used to make props for magicians including Ali Bongo, David Nixon, the Great Barnabus, Alan Alan and many others.'

'Really? What was his surname?' Rocco enquired.

'Wellbelove….Charlie Wellbelove.'

Greg Rocco shook his head.

'Might be a little bit before your time,' the Professor added.

'Maybe. Have you seen my act recently?'

They both shook their heads.

'Oh, I am at the ADC Theatre tomorrow night, I must give you two, complementary tickets.'

They both smiled appreciatively.

Rocco turned to the Professor.

'I don't use huge illusionary props and devices, like those your uncle built. My act is based around my birds which are very talented. I trained them myself. Do you want to come and meet them?"

The Professor nodded.

'Sorry, only one at a time. They are in the second bedroom,' he said to Roger. Rocco clearly attempting to exclude Philistines.

'No, worry. I need to talk with your neighbour. I will pop back in ten minutes,' Roger said.

 He smiled, walked back to the door and let himself out.

'Not sure he is a disciple for the Magic Circle,' Rocco sneared.

'Right, follow me into the room. Once in, stand absolutely still until my ladies get used to your presence and after that, no sudden movements,' he instructed.

111

The Professor nodded.

Rocco tapped lightly on the door and opened the door wide enough for his head to pass through the gap.

'Hello ladies, are you all okay?... Good...Don't be alarmed, I have a visitor come to see you. He is one of us,' he said in an almost childlike voice.

Without looking round he beckoned George to follow him into the room.

When George had shuffled through the gap, he found eight white doves on perches staring at him. Once he had become accustomed to the sight, he found it rather surreal and beautiful. There was no furniture in the room, apart from several bird cages, water bowls, a jug, several plastic tumblers and three large, black, rugged flight cases with the polished steel edges and corners - probably filled with stage props.

'Aren't they beautiful?' Rocco said in a loving, almost idolising voice.

The Professor had to admit that the collection of white doves was beautiful.

'You said you train them yourself?'

'Yes. Sometimes it takes three months to train a bird for a trick that lasts only ten seconds,' he smiled. 'It requires patience and dedication – but it is worth it. I will show you. '

He stretched out his arm and clicked his finger once. A white dove flew off its perch and landed on his wrist.

The sudden flutter of wings startled George.

'Sorry, I should have warned you,' Rocco apologised.

'This is Elizabeth,' he said stroking the bird's head and fussing under her chin, 'She's my super-star.'

The Professor edged closer - the bird cooed.

'She is a beautiful looking dove,' he complimented.

'Oh, she is not a dove, she is white pigeon.'

'Oh.'

'The others are doves. They are good for concealment in magic performances. Do you know they practically go to sleep when you tuck them in your jacket?'

'Yes, I had heard that.'

'But doves have no homing instinct. Release them into the wild and you may never see them again. Whereas Elizabeth is a star where that is concerned. When you come to the show tomorrow night you will see Elizabeth at her most brilliant. '

'Oh, yes, I'll be there. I love magic. Could my wife come too?'

'Oh yes, I will get you four complementary ticket - for you, your wife, your policeman friend and his partner.'

'That is very kind. We haven't been out to a theatre for months.'

Greg Rocco released the white pigeon who flew back to her perch.

'Now, Professor Wellbelove, you didn't come here to talk about magic. Shall we go back into the other room?'

As they returned to the lounge, he closed the door firmly and gestured to the sofa.

'Thank you,' the Professor said making himself comfortable.

'Now, Professor Wellbelove, what was it that you wanted to talk to me about?'

'Did you hear that Angela Galbraith's aunt died the other evening?'

'I am not here all the time, but I think I did hear something.'

'As Angela was the only person with her aunt all evening, she is regrettably the prime suspect.'

'Tragic turn of events,' he muttered.

'I can't believe that Angela is a murderess,' the Professor began. 'You know her better than I do, can you throw any light on to whether she is capable of killing or not?'

'As you said when you arrived, Angela and I were quite close once. I wanted desperately to make her part of my act. I could see a great future for us. But, she rejected me and my offer of employment,' he said bitterly. 'I guess that is a type of killing.'

He sighed loudly.

'Sorry, I must stop the theatrics, I'm not on stage at present.'

He looked across the lounge.

'To answer your question, yes, Angela can be a very selfish, single-minded lady – a real Quisling.'

The Professor nodded.

'She does appear all sweetness and light, but there is a determined girl beneath that.'

Greg Rocco didn't seem to want to add anymore to those words – he had said his piece.

'Oh right.'

Rocco rose to his feet. The Professor followed suit.

'Well, thank you for your thoughts ...and a glimpse of your beautiful birds.'

'You're very kind.....oh yes..'

Rocco rushed over to the dining table.

'Here are yours and your colleague's tickets for tomorrow night's show.'

The Professor took the tickets.

'You are very generous. I look forward to seeing your show,' he waved the tickets as he headed for the door. 'See you tomorrow night.'


The Professor found Roger three flats down the corridor.

'Here you are, two complimentary tickets to see Greg Rocco's performance in the Cabaret-Time Show tomorrow night at the ADC Theatre in Cambridge.'

'Wow,' Roger said taking his tickets. 'Are they freebies?'

'Rocco said they were complimentary.'

'That will be fabulous.'

'I am not getting very far with any of the residents – no one has seen anything. How did you get on with Rocco?'

'Not sure. I am going to have to sit down with a nice cup of tea and replay the conversation in my head.'

When the Professor arrived home, before he had a chance to even get to his study, the phone rang.

'How did you get on?' Peter's dulcet tones asked.

'Well, Roger and I met Greg Rocco. An odd showbiz guy with eight white birds.'

'With feathers, I assume?'

'Naturally.'

'Anything come to light?'

'Not really, I want to sit down with a cup of tea and go over the conversation again. There might be something, but I am not sure. Rocco called Angela a Quisling.'

'What's that in connection with?'

'I don't know.' The Professor puzzled. 'How did you get on with Rex Galbraith?'

'He admitted that Paul Knowles is his son.'

'Oh that's a result. Does it change anything?'

'Apparently Eleanor does know about it, so I guess there is some potency in the secret,' Peter concluded.

'Not to kill for,' George replied.

'No, Rex said the same.'

'We seem to keep coming back to this cross roads where we have a theory, but no evidence.'

'Yeah, I guess so,' Peter sighed. 'Anyway, I am having a day-off tomorrow, I am going fishing.'

'Good idea,' George replied, 'And Dorothy and I are going to the ADC Theatre to see a Cabaret Show including a magic show.'

'What Greg Rocco's?'

'Yep. He gave Roger and me, four complimentary tickets.'

'Oh you lucky devils. Perhaps I should have gone to Marlborough Court instead.'

'Until then, I am carriage clock repairing.'

'Okay, be in touch.

'Is he coming over?' Dorothy called from the kitchen with a fresh packet of digestive biscuits in her hand.

'No. So, one cup of tea and a plateful of biscuits in the study when you are ready, my love. Two cups if you would like to join me?'

'Oh you have such a way of sweeping a girl off her feet,' she grinned as she stroked her hair with her hand.

At seven o'clock Sunday evening, George and Dorothy were dressed up and ready to go to the theatre. It was only a short drive into the city, but parking might be difficult if they left it to the last minute. Plus, they could go in to the theatre and have a leisurely drink before the show.

The two settled in seats in the bar area and sipped their drinks.

'Oh I do like the sound of this Cabaret show, George. Do you think Greg Rocco will be good?' Dorothy asked.

'Well, it won't be lots of sawing ladies in half and people disappearing from cabinets, but his doves look quite beautiful. So I guess it will be lots of birds and sleight-of-hand magic.'

'Well, it's a night out ...and for free. It looks like quite a spectacular show.  Besides Greg Rocco, there are two musical groups, two singers, a comedian and some dancers. Sounds wonderful.'

At that moment Roger appeared. He had an attractive, blonde lady on his arm.

'Evening everybody,' he beamed. 'This is Ludmila. She is Polish.'

The slender young girl smiled and nearly curtsied.

'She doesn't speak very much English,' Roger apologised.

'Pleased to meet you,' she said awkwardly.

'What part of Poland are you from?' George asked with a polite smile.

She smiled back.

'Pleased to meet you,' she repeated.

'I think somewhere near Warsaw, George,' Roger said leaning over his shoulder.

'How do you converse?' George asked turning to Roger.

'We don't. We just smile a lot. Well, Ludmila giggles.'

'When did you meet her?'

'Last night at a club.'

'Well, I guess it is so noisy in these clubs, most people only smile and giggle anyway.'

George glanced over and could see Dorothy was chatting away to Ludmila.

'She doesn't know Polish, or does she?' he said to himself.

He leant across the table and Dorothy glanced round.

'She comes from a small village called Ostoja, near Szczecin on the Polish-German border.'

'How did you find that out?' he cried in amazement.

'I asked her...in German.'

'I didn't know you knew German?'

'Ja, mein guter Gefährte,' she chuckled. 'You must be confusing me with one of your other wives, George.'

'When did you learn that?'

'Oh, years ago, before I met you.'

'That was thirty years ago.'

'Just shows what a good memory I have.'

She turned and continued talking to Ludmila.

Roger returned from the bar with their drinks.

'Dorothy seems to be getting on well with Ludmila,,' he said.

'They are chatting in German,' George grunted.

'I didn't know Dorothy knew German?'

'No, nor did I,' said George. 'I guess, Roger, you can borrow her for dates. Then the two of you can progress from smiling and giggling.'

'Ladies and Gentlemen, 'the announcement speaker crackled into life, 'If you would take your seats, show-time will begin in ten minutes.'

'Right, time to go and watch the cabaret,' Dorothy said rising to her feet and grabbing George's arm. She was probably the most excited of the party to be at the theatre that evening.

'Down the side aisle on your left,' the smart young gentleman said as he glanced at their tickets.

They had the end four seats in the second row.

'Oh, these are lovely seat,' Dorothy enthused.

'Sehr gute Plätze,' Ludmila said to Roger, but he just smiled.

She turned to Dorothy and repeated the sentence.

'Yes,' Dorothy nodded.

'Very good seats, 'she called across to Roger, who smiled again.

'Oh, I am glad this is a show and not a meal,' Dorothy gasped to George.

The lights dimmed and with a crash of the cymbals, the stage filled with dancers. They were in semi-Latin costumes and got the show underway with a lively dance routine. This was followed by a rock group in smart black suits. Their appearance pleased the Professor, but the volume of their music didn't.

'Cover your ears,' Dorothy cried as she wriggled in her seat.

They only performed two numbers, which disappointed Dorothy, but pleased George.

The next act was a young female singer who had a voice not unlike Leona Lewis, George was informed by Dorothy. Her two songs were pleasant and George rather liked her.

'Ladies and Gentlemen,' the speakers boomed, 'meet the Deacon of Deliverance.'

The lights dimmed and all eyes focussed on the curtains at they parted. Centre stage stood a solitary figure in a black robe and hood lit by bright white light from behind. The music thundered out as his silhouette gyrated about the stage.

'Oh, is this Rocco?' Dorothy whispered.

'I guess so,' George replied. When he saw his ochre-coloured skin he would know.

The music came to a crescendo as he threw up his robe in a billowing expanse. The lights came up and Rocco's familiar face appeared.

'Yep, tangerine features,' George said to himself.

Rocco unclipped his robe and turned it inside out so he now wore a more virtuous white cloak.

'Good evening, ladies and gentlemen, my name is Rocco, Greg Rocco and I am going to entertain and baffle you over the next few minutes.'

His female assistant pushed out a clear plastic prop on a low stainless steel trolley to a place directly in front of Rocco.

It was basically two large square Perspex cones joined together at their points. The lower one forming the base, the upper one open into which the stage assistant was pouring water from a large glass jug.

A spotlight came on lighting the clear water.

The assistant handed Rocco a piece of red paper and a marker pen.

'Tonight, ladies and Gentlemen, you will witness something very uplifting and beautiful. Before your very eyes, I shall wash away one person's sins.'

George glanced across at Roger.

'Need him in the Police force,' he mouthed.

'I shall call upon Holy forces beyond this world to help someone to go forward from this day without the burden of guilt that they presently carry.'

Rocco stepped to the edge of the stage.

'I don't want anyone to tell me their sins, nor will they disclose them to the audience. They will write their sins – the sins that has been crippling them for years, on this piece of paper. Then I will call upon those Holy forces to expunge those sins.'

There was a loud titter in the audience.

'Who would like to place their conscience before the Holy forces and ask to be forgiven?'

Several hands shot up.

The Professor turned round and surveyed the volunteers. He wondered if Peter, with a polaroid camera, should have been there tonight - though most looked like impressionable housewives rather than axe-murderers.

'You madam,' Rocco pointed. 'Would you please come up onto the stage.'

A lady in her early forties in a black trouser suit pushed her way to the end of her row of seats and hurried to the steps that lead up on to the stage. Rocco stepped down one and held out his hand to guide the lady.

The lady looked rather delighted and embarrassed to be in the glare of the spotlights on the stage. She wriggled a little.

'Your name, madam? Just your first name, please?' Rocco asked.

'Julia,' she babbled

'Julia, you are carrying a terrible burden of something that you have done in your life that you regret? Something that is filling your conscience with guilt.'

Julia nodded.

Rocco's female assistant brought a small table onto the stage in front of her, as Rocco handed Julia the paper and pen.

'This is between you and your Maker, Julia. Please, Julia, write your sin on the piece of paper and fold it in half, so that no one, including myself will ever see the words. Only you and your Maker will know this transgression.'

He turned away and walked to behind the waist-high double cone.

The audience watched as Julia wrote something on the red sheet of paper, then folded it in half.

'Julia, please bring it here.'

Rocco took the folded sheet and, pushing up the sleeve of his jacket, he held the paper above his head.

Dark stirring music filled the theatre. The lights dimmed slightly. A single spot light picked out Rocco's hand and the piece of red paper. He placed his other hand on Julia's shoulder.

'I call upon the Holy forces that are around and with us this night, to look upon their daughter, Julia, with compassion. By writing her sin on this piece of paper, she has confessed and asked their forgiveness.'

The audience gulped.

There was a loud roll of the drums and suddenly Rocco's hand and the paper plunged into the clear water. All at once, the water turned pink. As he swished his hand around in the water the paper vanished and slowly the water turned back to clear again.

'The water is clear, ladies and gentlemen. It shows that the Holy forces have agreed and taken Julia's sins and purged them.'

There was a loud gasp and applause from the audience.

Julia burst into tears and threw her arms around the magician.

'Ladies and gentlemen, tonight you have witnessed a miracle with your own eyes. Julia, go forward, your conscience has been cleansed.'

There was a further almighty round of applause from the audience as Julia bowed to them and then threw her arms around Rocco again. He led her across the stage to the steps and with tears streaming down her cheeks, she returned to her seat.

'That was amazing,' Dorothy cried digging George's elbow.

George just smiled, so she turned to Ludmila and Roger and said the same.

George had seen a lot of magic when he was young and used to visit Uncle Charlie's workshop and view his latest contraption.

He knew many magician's tricks were remarkably simple, but it was their presentation and execution that separated the good from the exceptional. George had to admit, Rocco was pretty good.

While his assistant cleared the stage and brought on a pair of gleaming perches, Rocco began the magician's familiar movements of mis-direction as he began producing white doves out of thin air.

The audience clapped furiously.

His assistant finally brought on a white bird in a gold cage on a pedestal. She returned with a slender vase holding a single red carnation and placed it on the small table. As Rocco took the white bird out of its cage and began fussing it, the assistant removed the other white doves and their perches from the stage.

'Ladies and gentlemen this is the star of this evening, Elizabeth.'

He held the white bird aloft and she fluttered her wings as he lifted her into the air. He slowly brought her down, stoking her head as he did.

'Is there any lady in the audience, who *doesn't* like receiving flowers?' he joked.

'Can I have the house lights up a shade?' he requested.

The theatre audience, most blinking from the light, came into view.

Rocco walked to the edge of the stage with Elizabeth at the end of his outstretched arm.

'I need another volunteer.' He gazed around and then pointed to a lady in the centre, about ten rows back.

'You, madam. Can you stand up please?' he said genially.

The lady in a white jacket and white skirt stood up.

'Excellent,' Rocco complimented. 'Your name madam?'

'Diane.'

'Thank you, Diane.'

'You are not afraid of birds or of a nervous disposition?'

'No,' she grinned.

'Good. And you like flowers?'

'Oh yes,' she beamed.

'Good.'

Rocco turned to the white bird in his hand.

'That is Diane,' Rocco said softly to the bird as he pointed with his other hand.

'Diane, please remain standing and hold one arm up and across your chest, please. Just as you do when you fold your arms, but this time with just one arm. Out a bit further. Yes, that's it.'

Rocco walked back to centre stage and lowered the white bird so that its beak nearly touched the red carnation. He then walked over to the side of the stage.

There was a roll of the drums.

'Fly, my beauty,' he cried as he launched Elizabeth in to the air. She flew over to the small table and landed briefly. She took hold of the stem of the red carnation with her beak and launched herself into the air again - this time firmly holding the carnation. She swooped across the stage and out in to the auditorium. There was a loud gasp from the audience as the bird soared over their heads and headed for Diane, who looked a little apprehensive.

'Stand absolutely still, Diane,' Rocco instructed.

The bird and carnation landed on Diane's arm.'

'Please take the carnation, Diane.'

As she did, the bird launched herself into the air and flew back to Rocco and his outstretched arm in the centre of the stage.

'Diane, with my compliments,' Rocco called out as he bowed, the audience clapped and Diane went pink.

'That was a lovely act, George,' Dorothy declared. She turned, but George was miles away.

Before Dorothy had much time to discuss the act further, cheery music heralded the entrance of the comedian with an oversized jacket and loud tie.

'Evening all,' he cried and peered down at the audience.

'God, the Salvation Army hostel full tonight?' he cried to shrieks from the audience.

'I said the hostel full, grandpa? Not brought your hearing aid with you tonight? Anyone in here do that funny sign language?' and he proceeded to do grossly exaggerated hand movements ending up with his back to the audience and his arms between his legs. The audience loved his repartee.

'Psssst. Roger, 'George called quietly.

'Outside,' he gestured furiously.

'You leaving?' the comedian called out to George and Roger as they pushed along the row. 'I normally insult someone, but not usually this early in the act.'

George ignored the remarks as he gathered Roger and pushed him through the swing doors.

'I think I know how the poison bottle vanished,' George exploded.

'Did you have to drag me out of the show to tell me that?' Roger said angrily.

'You need to go round to Greg Rocco's apartment while we know for certain that he is here at the theatre, He's got a second performance in forty minutes' time.'

'Now?' Roger protested.

'Yes, right now. I am going to phone Peter and get him to organise the search warrant. Then the two of us will meet you there.'

'What about the ladies?'

'Dorothy can take the car and she will get Ludmila home.'

'Roger, take a uniformed officer with you, time is of the essence. But pick him up, I don't want a huge white patrol car in the visitors' bay at Marlborough Court when Rocco returns home.'

Roger shook his head, but headed for the exit.

'Peter, it is George............'

After hurriedly explaining to the ladies what was happening and receiving yet more abuse from the comedian, George waited on the pavement outside the theatre for Peter's car.

'I was in the middle of my pizza when you phoned,' Peter greeted his friend.'

'Sorry about that,' the Professor said climbing into the car.

'I do hope you know what you are doing, George,' the Chief Inspector continued to reprimand his colleague. 'Despatching two of my police officers to break into a person's flat is considerably outside the job spec of a university lecturer.'

'Even for solving a murder enquiry?'

The Chief Inspector huffed.

'You do try my patience, George.'

'You've got the search warrant?' George asked.

'That's another person you've upset. Yes, of course I have.'

The Chief Inspector's mobile phone rang. He glanced at the screen.

'Roger,' he said to the Professor.

'Roger, how's it going?'

'Sir, we're in Rocco's flat. We didn't have to start going through the cupboards or anything. We went into his bedroom.....sir, you have got to see this.'

'Roger, stay put, we are a couple of minutes away.'

He hung up and glanced at the Professor.

'Looks like your little hunch is paying off, George.'

When they arrived at Marlborough Court, the Chief Inspector pulled in alongside Roger's car in the visitors' parking bay -they were both unmarked police vehicles, so there was no problem.

The two hurried up to the third floor and Greg Rocco's flat. They rang the bell and a uniformed officer answered the door.

'Evening, sir. Sergeant Carter is in there,' he pointed.

The Chief Inspector and the Professor strode across the lounge and into the main bedroom.

'Oh my god,' Peter cried.

'Oh, he has got it bad,' George added.

The three looked down on Greg Rocco's bedside cabinet. There was one large framed photograph of Angela Galbraith, four smaller ones, including her in her stage costume, some dried roses, a couple of letters and the centre-piece - a green peridot earring on a white satin cushion.

'Is that the one she thought she had lost?' the Chief Inspector enquired.

But he really didn't need to ask.

The Chief Inspector then looked at the other photograph on the other bedside cabinet.

'Who's that?' he asked.

'I think you will find that is Tony Warlock,' said the Professor.

'I assume that is stage blood all over his photograph?'

'But the dagger through the eye is quite real,' George gulped.

'The guy has got a screw loose,' the Chief Inspector growled,

'Obsession coupled with anger. Now, that's an explosive mixture. Signing with Tony Warlock was clearly the last straw for Rocco,' George said as he shook his head. 'Rocco used a rather unusual word *Quisling* when he referred to Angela.'

'A traitor,' the Chief Inspector stated.

'That's it. Angela had betrayed him.'

The Chief Inspector turned and gazed at the modern-day shrine coupled with the equivalent of an effigy with pins in it.

'Sir,' the uniformed officer called, 'I found this on the kitchen window ledge.'

He handed the Chief Inspector a small spiral bound notebook.

The Chief Inspector opened it and began reading.

'More damning evidence?' the Professor asked.

'Oh, yes. It is in a shorthand code, but I guess it is all the movements across the way in Angela's flat.'

He held the page open for the Professor to see. Down the left hand side of the page was a column of times. Against each was an entry like "M -> K"; "A & M – Lunch".

'I assume "M" for Margaret, "A" for Angela and "K" is kitchen etc. ?' said the Professor.

'I found these in a kitchen drawer,' the uniformed officer said as he handed the Chief Inspector a pair of binoculars.

'A static stalker,' said the Chief Inspector. 'Our friend has clearly been watching the flat for quite a few days. I guess he knows their routine pretty accurately.'

'Hold on, what was Rocco's motive for killing Margaret Knowles?'

'Everything and nothing,' replied the Professor. 'Shall I tell you what happened last Tuesday?'

'Please do.'

'Greg Rocco was bitterly angry that Angela Galbraith had dumped him as a boyfriend. He might be able to cope with that and possibly win her back, if she had agreed to be his stage assistant. He tried for months to woo her with flowers. Finally, just before her skiing holiday, she signed with Tony Warlock. That was the breaking point. If Rocco couldn't have her, no one else would. His deep love turned to bitter hatred. As Roger and I saw this evening, Rocco has a white homing pigeon who can fly out and fly back, I think that is the technical term for it. It is quite rare, but he has trained his bird, Elizabeth to do that.

When I was talking to Jack Glover, he told me that he had found paper fibres in Margaret's glass together with a tiny triangle of Sellotape.'

The Chief Inspector frowned. He was finding it difficult to keep up with the Professor's mind that could leap from factor to factor.

'Tonight, Roger and I witnessed Rocco using water soluble paper in his act – dip it in water and it completely decomposes in seconds.'

The Chief Inspector nodded.

'I believe Rocco had watched Angela's flat for many days and nights – he knew their routine intimately. Last Tuesday the days was hot and the night warm. Angela and Margaret had the patio doors wide open. The stage was set.

After pouring out the drinks, Angela said that Margaret helped her to the toilet.'

The Chief Inspector nodded.

'They were only away for a couple of minutes, but time enough for Rocco to act. He had everything prepared and ready to go. He soaked some of his water-soluble paper with concentrated aconite. He carefully affixed the Sellotape triangle on one corner.'

'Sorry, George, what does that do?'

'Bird's beaks are not permeable, Peter, but Rocco was not taking any chance. He wanted to make sure that his prized bird, Elizabeth didn't get any poison on her beak or in her mouth.'

'R-i-g-h-t.'

'As Margaret and Angela disappeared into the bathroom, Rocco despatched Elizabeth with her deadly offering. She had flown across to the flat before. Remember, she had done that journey before when she delivered red roses to Angela?'

'Oh yes, her mother told us about that stunt,' Peter grinned.

'The bird delivered the aconite soaked paper into the glass.'

'Which dissolved immediately,' Peter said as the revelation struck home. Then a further though struck him.

'But the glass wasn't full of water.'

'No, vodka and bitter lemon. Eighty proof vodka is about sixty percent water. That was a stoke of good fortune for Rocco. Aconite won't dissolve in water - it needs alcohol. The special paper is the reverse – it needs water. Margaret's drink was the perfect cocktail with both elements.'

'So, no poison bottle?' the Chief Inspector frowned.

'No, never was one in Angela's flat.'

'No, "Man or Lady in the Corridor"?'

'Didn't exist.'

'And the Galbraith / Knowles conspiracy theory?'

'Just a passing theory,' George smiled.

'George, this has to be one of the most convoluted mysteries that you and I have ever faced.'

'I think so.'

The huge smile on the Chief Inspector's face evaporated.

'Hold on,' he said, staring at his colleague. 'You have just detailed how Rocco planned to kill Angela Galbraith, but it is Margaret Knowles's murder that we are dealing with.'

'*A tragic turn of events* as Greg Rocco said to me only yesterday. It took me ages to realise the significance of those words.'

'*A tragic turn of events?* You've lost me,' said the Chief Inspector.

'Because his beloved white pigeon, Elizabeth put the poison in the wrong glass - Margaret's and not Angela's.'

As the Professor uttered the words, there was the sound of a key turning in the lock. Greg Rocco opened the door. His initial expression of surprise at seeing his flat full of police officers turned to realisation, then resignation – the game was up.

# THE END

Printed in Great Britain
by Amazon